Barbara Zahn

BOOKS BY
EMILIE LORING

THE TRAIL OF CONFLICT
HERE COMES THE SUN!
A CERTAIN CROSSROAD
THE SOLITARY HORSEMAN
GAY COURAGE
SWIFT WATER
LIGHTED WINDOWS
FAIR TOMORROW
UNCHARTED SEAS
HILLTOPS CLEAR
WE RIDE THE GALE!
WITH BANNERS
IT'S A GREAT WORLD
GIVE ME ONE SUMMER
AS LONG AS I LIVE
TODAY IS YOURS
HIGH OF HEART
ACROSS THE YEARS
THERE IS ALWAYS LOVE
WHERE BEAUTY DWELLS
STARS IN YOUR EYES
RAINBOW AT DUSK
WHEN HEARTS ARE LIGHT AGAIN
KEEPERS OF THE FAITH
BEYOND THE SOUND OF GUNS
BRIGHT SKIES
BECKONING TRAILS
I HEAR ADVENTURE CALLING
LOVE CAME LAUGHING BY
TO LOVE AND TO HONOR
FOR ALL YOUR LIFE
MY DEAREST LOVE
I TAKE THIS MAN
THE SHADOW OF SUSPICION
WHAT THEN IS LOVE
LOOK TO THE STARS
BEHIND THE CLOUD
WITH THIS RING
HOW CAN THE HEART FORGET
THROW WIDE THE DOOR
FOLLOW YOUR HEART
A CANDLE IN HER HEART
FOREVER AND A DAY
SPRING ALWAYS COMES
A KEY TO MANY DOORS
IN TIMES LIKE THESE

IN TIMES LIKE THESE

IN TIMES
LIKE THESE

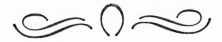

EMILIE LORING

LITTLE, BROWN AND COMPANY
BOSTON • TORONTO

Published simultaneously in Canada
by Little, Brown & Company (Canada) Limited

PRINTED IN THE UNITED STATES OF AMERICA

IN TIMES LIKE THESE

"WILL Miss Wilburn come to Mr. Markham's office at once, please?"

Page Wilburn looked up from the shorthand notes over which she was frowning. Markham? What on earth did the big boss want with her? Then she gathered up notebook and pencils and walked swiftly across the office, took the elevator to the top floor, went down the long hall to the suite of offices which was the domain of Horace Markham, head of the Markham Electronics Company and so important that, as a rule, only the top brass ever caught sight of him.

Although Page had worked six months for the organization she had never seen him except in newspaper pictures, talking with the President of the United States, with visiting dignitaries from foreign nations, with other men who lived on his own exalted level.

When she opened the door marked *Horace Markham, President,* a smiling and alert secretary said, "Miss Wilburn? Go right in. Mr. Markham is expecting you."

For a moment as she entered the room she blinked, her eyes dazzled by the brilliant San Francisco sunlight, by the glittering waters of the bay. Her eyes were caught by the soaring Golden Gate Bridge and then she turned away reluctantly from the great sweep of the window, which filled a whole wall, to face the two men who had risen as she went in. They were not sitting at Markham's big, polished desk but in easy chairs near the window with its spectacular view.

Markham she recognized at once, the big leonine head of white hair, the eyes made startling by the bushy black brows, the hard line of the jaw. The other man was slighter, the curl of his dark mahogany hair was firmly disciplined. He was perhaps thirty, with the relaxed air of a man very much at home in his world, a man who had no quarrel with it, a man who believed he could handle whatever came his way. In other words, he had all the qualities that were most unlike the girl that Page Wilburn had become in recent months.

"Miss Wilburn," Markham said, after summing her up in a long look, with just a shade of disappointment in his expression, "this is an old friend of mine, Vance Cooper, from our New York office, who expects to spend a week in San Francisco and needs someone to do personal work for him. I have suggested that you give him a helping hand."

"Of course," Page said in the colorless voice that had been hers for the past six months. Her voice was as dull as Page herself, her body shapeless in the heavy mourning she wore, her mouth and cheeks pale, her eyes downcast. Even the heavy, honey-colored hair was drawn back so tightly one could almost feel the pull, and fastened in a big knot at the back of her head.

Behind the expressionless face — expressionless, that is, except for the bitterness of the mouth — a quick mind was at work. A man in Markham's position did not have direct dealings with minor clerical workers. Why had she been singled out to work with the confident young man with the mahogany hair? She took the chair Vance Cooper pulled up for her and waited passively.

"Mr. Cooper," Markham said, "needs someone to do a highly confidential job." He caught Page's eyes and held them. "So important, Miss Wilburn, that if it were to be known to the wrong people it could do incalculable harm." When she made no reply he said, an edge of impatience on his voice, "You understand that?"

"Oh, yes, I understand. What I do not understand —"

"Well?"

"Why me?" she asked. "You have nearly seven thousand employees here. Why take a chance on me for something so important?"

Markham seemed oddly disconcerted. At length he said, "Sometimes I think so-called loyalty clearances are rather like intelligence tests. They cannot possibly show what one will do, only what his potentialities are. I am putting my faith in the fact that you are Hank Wilburn's daughter."

Page's head jerked up in surprise. Whatever she had expected it had not been that.

"Hank was the closest I ever came to having a brother. Even when his job took him to South America we never lost touch. When I learned of his death I tried to trace his family. You had lost your mother and you had come back to the United States. In fact, you were living right here in San Francisco. I believe you came because your fiancé lives here."

Page's hands gripped the arms of her chair. It did not seem possible that she could grow any paler.

Markham watched her. "I wrote to you, offering any assistance in my power. You replied that you were going to be married and that you would be taken care of. You needed nothing. Then, quite by chance, during one of those periodical loyalty check-ups of our personnel, I saw your name among our employees."

He looked down at the slender hands holding so tightly to the chair arms. On the ring finger of the left hand there was a paler mark where a ring had been.

She watched him. Something about her frozen quiet made the younger man stir uneasily in his chair.

At last she said, "I — am not going to be married, Mr. Markham."

"Tell me," he said in an easy, conversational tone, "why, if you refused my help, you came to work with this company?"

Seeing the intent eyes of the two men, she was aware that they attached a great deal of importance to her answer.

"I didn't want any — favoritism," she said at last. "The husband of one of my friends is in this office and the fiancé of another has been transferred to the New York office. They both told me you were fair to your employees, that your treatment of them was generous, and that I would be happy here." Again her mouth betrayed an underlying bitterness.

"I hope you agree with them," Markham said with a smile.

"Everyone has been helpful." The colorless voice revealed no feeling.

Markham looked down at the motionless girl. "What it comes to is this, Miss Wilburn. Once I wanted to help you if I could and you refused. Now I want, I very much want, you to help me. Will you refuse again?"

"Do I have the choice?" Her voice was hostile.

"Of course you have the choice. Your job will be in no

way imperiled if you refuse. All I ask, in that case, is that you forget whatever you have been told here."

"That, of course, you may rely on."

"Then you intend to refuse?"

"I don't know, because I don't understand what you require of me."

"There are thousands and thousands of people today, Miss Wilburn, who are taking risks, enormous risks, to help their country, even when they know only one small fraction of the problem. They take things on faith."

"Like my father," she said bitterly.

"Like your father. It was Hank's faith in his fellowmen, his undeviating faith in good, that made him so magnificent a human being."

"It also made him a failure," Page replied. "If you followed his career you must know that by the time he died he had been stripped of everything except a few hundred dollars."

"A failure!" There was anger in Markham's voice. "I did not realize that your estimate of your father was based on the size of his estate." He pushed back his chair. "I was mistaken in you, Miss Wilburn. I think there is nothing more to be said."

"Wait!" She flung out her hand. "I am ashamed. Of course he wasn't a failure. He was wonderful and I was always proud of him. I was just angry because life was so unfair to him."

Markham stood up. "He didn't think so."

"I know." Page's voice was husky. "He thought living was a wonderful adventure and a challenge. He always said that what counted was running the race, not just the winning. He always said it wasn't important to get ahead of other people — that what mattered was getting ahead of yourself, using all you have, not wasting your talents or your energy."

Markham studied her for a moment. "Then perhaps, if you shared any of your father's ideas, you would like to have a week in which to make your decision about my proposition, Miss Wilburn."

The younger man had not spoken at all. He went to open the door for Page; his manner was impeccably courteous, but the lines at the corners of his mouth betrayed him. From the moment when she had spoken bitterly of her father's failure he had been disgusted. She saw his expression, flushed hotly, turned back from the door.

"I don't need a week in which to make my decision, Mr. Markham," she said crisply. "I'll do that job for you."

ii

"With all the girls in the world to choose from," Vance Cooper said in disgust when Page had gone, "why did you have to pick that particular one?"

"You heard me tell her why. I knew her father who was, beyond comparison, the finest man I ever met. From what he used to write me of his daughter, she is cut out of the same cloth. I can remember his writing once that she had an understanding heart, that she had the rare gift of being able to help people without appearing to criticize."

"You are taking a parent's estimate of his own child. As a rule, parents are the poorest, the most prejudiced, judges."

"That is probably true in most cases but, you see, I knew Hank."

"It struck me," the young man remarked, "that his

daughter didn't even seem to like him much, let alone resemble him."

Markham shook his head. "She adored him. What embittered her, and I grant that she is embittered now, is that he trusted a friend who cheated him out of practically everything he had."

"So she couldn't forgive him," Vance said unsympathetically, "for losing his money. Now isn't that just too bad."

"You are wrong, Vance."

"And that mourning. For my money it is straight hypocrisy."

"The mourning, I suspect, is her way of standing by to repel invaders : a 'keep off' sign."

Vance laughed. "She's the last girl on earth who needs to worry. I can't imagine any man bothering to take a second look at her. She's going to a lot of trouble for nothing."

Markham studied the younger man thoughtfully for a moment. "I told you I checked her out thoroughly. While she was in Peru with her father she became engaged to a young man from San Francisco. After her father's death she came up here to join her fiancé. When I wrote, offering any assistance I could give her, everything seemed to be all right for her. She told me how grateful she was but said that she needed nothing as she was going to marry— uh, what was his name? Oh, yes, Jerome Brooks. But Brooks seems to be a young man who keeps his eye on the main chance. When Hank was proved to have lost his money — and at one time he had a lot of it — Brooks promptly lost interest in the girl."

"That fast?" Vance was startled.

"That fast. He broke off with her, a nice, clean, quick

operation. No chloroform. Told her the blunt truth. That is, if I have heard the story correctly. He 'couldn't afford' to jeopardize his future in the diplomatic service by marrying a woman without enough money to be an adequate hostess."

"Oh, I see."

"So she doesn't like or trust men, that's about the size of it," Markham concluded. "What's bothering you, Vance?"

"It seems to me that you are taking the girl on trust solely on the basis of your admiration for her father. Children don't always inherit their parents' good qualities. I could tell you of a case from my personal experience." Vance broke off for a moment and then went on. "If this Page Wilburn has grown into a bitter, discontented woman, who is to say that she has not become vindictive and revengeful? We know she has no money. We know she resents her father for losing his money."

"Meaning just what?" Markham demanded.

"Meaning," the younger man said, "that she may have taken the job here, or been planted here, because there is a lot of important information to be gathered."

Momentarily Markham looked troubled; then he shook his head. "No," he said with decision. "She refused my help, both financial and personal. She took this job without informing me so as not to appear to ask for my influence, to progress as she could on her own merits."

"We'll hope you are right, sir."

"I am sure that I am right about this." Markham was amused. "When the well-being of this country is at stake I take no chances. I've had an unobtrusive eye on Miss Wilburn ever since you suggested your plan. I'll continue to have one. It may be unobtrusive, but it is very observant."

"At least," Vance insisted, "it would do no harm to find out what friends suggested that Miss Wilburn work for Markham, after she refused your help."

"We'll do that, of course. The big snag, I'm afraid, will come when she learns exactly what you expect of her. At this moment — of course, she's too young for such a situation to last — she dislikes and distrusts men."

After a moment of thought Vance said cheerfully, "Well, to be quite cold-blooded about it, that makes the whole situation ideal for me."

"You are assuming then that she will go through with the deal after she understands the conditions."

"Why not?" Vance asked reasonably. "There is no personal issue at stake, thank God! Not with a girl who is about as alluring as a moth-eaten old fur piece. She will get a month's vacation with all expenses paid in New York, a complete wardrobe — and, from what I've seen, she could use one. She will also receive a bonus of five thousand dollars. All she has to do for that is to pretend, for four short weeks, that she is engaged to marry me. What does she have to lose?"

Markham stared out of the window. However often he saw that fabulous view, particularly on a clear day when San Francisco air sparkles and you can see forever, it never lost its power to exalt him. But now he was troubled.

"Hank Wilburn was my valued friend. I begin to think I don't like this setup, Vance. I simply can't stand back and let the girl be endangered, even in a good cause."

"She won't be endangered." The young man was amused. "Certainly not by me. And she'll be staying with

my Aunt Jane, who is a monument of respectability, Social
Register, all that. I can't conceive of her making the slightest compromise with her principles."

"Frankly," Markham admitted, "I fail to understand
why you need to have this girl provided, or any girl for that
matter."

"Because of Beverly Main. I thought I had explained all
that. She is my aunt's goddaughter and she is planning to
move in on Aunt Jane. For some eight years my aunt has
been trying to marry me off to a suitable girl — suitable to
her, that is. Then Beverly began to cultivate her. It's a
queer situation, Mr. Markham. Because of my job, I automatically had a check put on her when she began to hover
around Aunt Jane so persistently. After all, my aunt hadn't
seen the girl since she was five years old. At this time,
when we are on the lookout for any odd situation, I got interested in the sudden emergence of Beverly. Of course, it
may simply be that she wants to dig herself in on my aunt's
good graces. Aunt Jane is a wealthy woman. But there is a
lot of fog in the girl's background, so much that I begin to
wonder whether she actually is the girl she claims to be."

"Planted, you mean?" Markham asked with sudden interest.

Vance shook his head helplessly. "I just don't know.
The reports aren't all in yet. It's a kind of feeling. Anyhow,
there is only one guestroom in my aunt's little house in New
York City, and I want to get someone settled in it before
Beverly can do any harm."

"Such as?"

"Well, she seems to have an unusual amount of curiosity.
While she was weekending there not long ago, I caught her
trying to overhear my telephone conversations, my bureau

drawers and briefcase and desk were searched, and at least one letter addressed to me at my aunt's house was steamed open. Naturally there was nothing to find. I'm not that careless."

"But if she's not the girl she claims to be, she must be carefully briefed about your background and your aunt's, and this Beverly Main's as well. Who would be in a position to do that?"

Vance shook his head without speaking and Markham's eyes narrowed. For the first time in a long and satisfactory business relationship he felt that the young man was being less than frank with him. He started to speak, changed his mind.

"What I can't figure out," he said with a faint grin, "is why a man like you, who is not altogether repulsive to look at and who has climbed as high as you have as fast as you have, can't supply a girl of his own."

"I'm not trying to be melodramatic, sir, or to play this up," Vance said, "but I've had a feeling for some time that I am trailed wherever I go. Whoever has been doing it, if it is being done, must realize that I am not particularly serious about any special girl in New York." He laughed. "For one thing, you keep me too darned busy. But, as I am out here so often, I could produce a San Francisco girl without arousing any suspicion."

"Just the same," Markham said uneasily, "I wish it didn't have to be the daughter of my old friend."

Vance laughed. "So do I. Aunt Jane is no gullible fool. She is going to wonder what on earth attracted me to a girl like that and steered me away from a glamour girl like her goddaughter."

"Glamour?"

Vance whistled expressively.

Markham glanced at his watch, a reminder that his time was valuable. "All right, my boy, now what about Operation Homebase?"

Vance talked rapidly, without relying on notes. He had lived with this project for nearly five years; lived with it, slept with it, dreamed of it. The Markham Electronics Company was at work on a hush-hush program. If they made the breakthrough, of which they were now fairly confident and on which they had spent enormous sums of money, there would be a tremendous difference in the space race. Naturally, everyone involved had been checked and double-checked. But somehow, through some source, information had leaked out. The possibility remained that more information, perhaps decisive information, might follow the same route.

Vance had come out to the West Coast from the New York office, as he frequently did, to confer with Markham, as they were the only men who held all the strings in their hands, who knew all the facts. The appropriate government agencies had done what they could to stop leaks, to dig out undesirable employees, but the thing went on.

"So what it boils down to is that we have no clue at all to where the leak is," Vance said gloomily.

"One thing is fairly clear." Markham was grim. His great leonine head looked as though he were about to pounce. "We've been careful about how much information reached any single individual. For anything of major importance to get through, and we know from what trickled back to us from East Berlin that it has got through, we have a traitor somewhere near the top."

"How do you think it is being handled?"

"The material is being microfilmed and sent out of the country by courier."

"But how is it done?" This time it was Vance Cooper who had the impression that Markham was not being completely frank with him.

"So far as I can figure it, there is no open meeting between the courier and the person who passes on the information. They work through an intermediary who recognizes the courier by a password. My informant has learned that much. Time for lunch. Come on. Let's go to the Mark Hopkins. We need a break."

"First," Vance said, "I'd like to share your faith in this — what's her odd name? — Page Wilburn. I'd like to have a complete new security check made on her. I'd like to know who her friends at Markham are. And I'd like to know whether she has come into any money recently. Someone is paying out a lot of money for those microfilms, and couriers come high. It's a risky job, after all."

"We'll check," Markham assured him. "The trouble is, from what we can figure out, not only that a different courier is used each time but that the courier is sent to a different country."

Vance grinned. "I won't admit that the enemy can work out a trick we can't detect. We're going to stop this thing."

"God grant you are right," Markham said fervently.

TWO

"HEAVENS, it's one-thirty," Page exclaimed in distress. "I'm expected back at the office at one o'clock. I don't keep executive hours."

"Perhaps you will when this new assignment you've been telling me about comes through."

Page smiled mockingly at Leslie Trevor. Mrs. Gordon Trevor, social leader, the best-dressed woman in San Francisco, married to a prosperous lawyer who adored her, knew nothing about the problems of a working girl.

"Go ahead and laugh at me." Leslie was unperturbed. "But do you know something, Page? You are turning your back on life at twenty-three, and that's a crime against human nature."

"Don't!" Page said in a choked voice.

Leslie slipped her hand under her friend's arm — the arm was too thin, too tense — and turned her around so that they saw their reflections in a store window. "Look at yourself! You've just given up. I'm ashamed of you. You've packed up your life and put it away in mothballs. You are turning into a different person. Remember all the years while we were growing up — Alice and Helen and you and I — it was always you who provided a . . . a kind of balance wheel for the rest of us. We depended on you to keep our values clear, to give us courage when we lacked it. We . . . need you, Page. Lots of people need someone like you.

Sometimes I think neither Alice nor Helen would have made such a mess of things if you hadn't been in Peru."

"What do you expect me to do?"

"For one thing, get out of that mourning. Your father loved bright colors."

"But he has been dead only a few months. Anyhow —"

"Anyhow, be honest with yourself, darling. You aren't in mourning for your father; it's for Jerry."

"Leslie!" Page jerked away from her, cheeks blazing.

"Take it easy, sweetie. Even if I make you hate me, I've got to shake some sense into you, make you look at things honestly. You slink along the streets afraid to look up for fear you will come across Jerry at the next corner. You deliberately make yourself look as unattractive as you can. You wear mourning to warn every man who looks at you: Keep off."

"Well —"

"You are twenty-three," Leslie stormed at her. "Your life isn't over. Why it hasn't even begun. All right, I'll agree that Jerry was every kind of a rat —"

"Please!" Page flung out a black-gloved hand, imploring her friend to be silent.

Leslie shook her head. "No, I've kept still for months, while I've watched you dwindle into something practically invisible in the background, all because a selfish man loved himself more than he did you. I'm ashamed of you, Page. And what's more, your father would be ashamed. He took a lot of blows, but he was never bitter and he never stopped believing that life was good."

"He was cheated," Page said stubbornly.

"Not of the real things. And at least he didn't cheat himself, as you are cheating yourself. He met every adventure head-on and enjoyed it to the hilt as experience. Even when he got hurt. It's better to be hurt than just to be numb. Believe me, Page!"

Page was silent. Leslie looked at her uneasily. "You aren't angry with me?"

"Not with you. Never with you, Leslie. What would people do without real friends to be honest with them? No, I'm angry with myself. I believe you are right."

Her friend expelled a long breath of relief. "Then, Page, will you agree to do one thing for me?"

Page hesitated and then nodded.

"Good. I want you to get out of that mourning and into bright colors. You'll be amazed at what they can do for you. They will lift your spirits the way the sun does after a long period of fog and rain."

"But I — perhaps later."

"You mean you can't afford to buy new clothes now, don't you?" Leslie was blunt. "I realize it must take all you earn to keep you. Will you, stubborn friend and stingy receiver that you are, let me have the pleasure of doing just this one thing? Let me buy you one complete outfit. Please!"

"Then — yes, Leslie, I'd be delighted."

"What color?" her friend asked, trying to conceal her pleasure.

Page turned her head. "Oh —" she said on a long breath.

San Francisco is the proud possessor of one of the most beautiful shops in the world, a shop with a heavy and ugly name that sounds like a loud thump. Gump's. In it is one of the finest collections of jade to be found anywhere.

Page stared into one of the windows. "Jade is really the miracle stone, isn't it?" she said softly. "Exquisite to the eye, lovely to the touch. You can have all the diamonds in the world. I'll take jade any time."

As usual, people had stopped to look in the window. Reflected in the glass, Page could see a drab woman in a brown coat, a woman who was extremely overweight; a ferret-faced man who looked as though he never had a square meal; Leslie Trevor, as smart as only the great dressmakers can make a woman; and herself draped in heavy mourning.

"How about jade-green?" Leslie asked. "At least for accessories. That should be wonderful with your coloring."

"I'd love it." Somewhere a clock chimed and Page said hastily, "I must get back. Mr. Markham may be expecting me. Thank you for the lunch, for the scolding, for everything."

But it was not until late the next morning that she was summoned again to Horace Markham's office. This time the eyes of the other clerks followed her in surprise. To forestall speculation she said, "I'm to do some work for a man from the New York office."

"If it's the one who was in the elevator with Mr. Markham yesterday," one of the girls commented, "the good-looking one with the dark red hair, tell him I'll do the job for nothing."

Page laughed but made no reply. The door of Markham's office was open and his secretary nodded for her to go in. This time she was prepared to encounter Vance Cooper, the man from New York who had revealed his disapproval of her the day before.

When they had exchanged good mornings Markham said, "Miss Wilburn, Mr. Cooper has a suggestion to make

which would require you to go to New York for a month.
If you agree, you will receive a five-thousand-dollar bonus
for the job as well as your usual salary and all expenses.
You will not, of course, inform anyone — *anyone* — of
the reason for your trip to New York or its probable du-
ration. In fact, we would prefer not to have you say that you
are going on an assignment for us. If possible, draw on
your own imagination for a sound reason for getting an indefinite leave of absence, but something that could be
checked out if anyone should happen to be curious."

New York! New York and a mysterious assignment.
This was adventure with a vengeance.

"Mr. Cooper will explain the job to you," Markham
went on. "As I said yesterday, you are under no compul-
sion to accept, none whatever, and I will neither recom-
mend it nor attempt to persuade you. In fact, I won't even
try to take advantage of your impulsive statement yesterday. You need not make up your mind immediately. You
aren't being rushed into anything, you know. Mr. Cooper
will be here for another six days."

Later, Page was to remember with wry amusement
Markham's additional comment, "I must say you look
tired; a change might be the best thing for you. You'll find
it restful."

Restful!

Cooper addressed her for the first time. "Will you lunch
with me, Miss Wilburn, while we talk it over?"

"Take off the rest of the day," Markham suggested. "I'll
have my secretary explain to your department manager."

So Page found herself lunching with Vance Cooper. Until they had ordered, he talked easily of impersonal matters, of travel and staying at home; of San Francisco, one

of the few cities with a proud individuality of its own; of sports and theater and music. Somewhat to her surprise, Page found herself relaxed and interested. For the first time since her engagement had been so cruelly broken, she was too occupied to look around a restaurant in terror of encountering Jerry.

When at last she did look around casually she was not even thinking of him. Her eyes wandered from table to table, went back to a man who seemed vaguely familiar. It was the ferret-faced man whose reflection she had seen in Gump's window, and she was glad to discover that she had been mistaken about his not having enough to eat. He was tackling a large meal with enthusiasm, looking up now and then as though to nod agreement to someone across the table. The other person was not visible from where Page sat.

It was a restaurant with that increasingly rare luxury, tables widely enough spaced so that people can talk without being overheard or overhearing. When the waiter had served the soup and gone, Cooper said, "I don't suppose you know much about the work being done at Markham Electronics."

"Not a thing," Page admitted. "I'm not an engineer, of course, just a stenographer. Frankly, I don't even know the meaning of half the words that are dictated to me and, besides, they aren't top-secret stuff — mostly office management and that sort of thing."

Cooper took a quick look around, said with lowered voice, "Have you ever heard of Operation Homebase?"

She shook her head, and he wished that the dark glasses did not conceal her eyes. It is difficult to assess a person's character or mentality when the eyes are hidden.

"We have something very big, Miss Wilburn, big enough to alter our history, if we don't lose it to the enemy."

"That important?"

"That important," Cooper assured her. "Now here is where you come in. Our major work will be finished within a month if all goes well, but for that length of time we have to stop every conceivable leak."

"There is a leak?" Page was startled.

He nodded. "Someone high up," he said, anger in his voice. "Someone in the New York area. At least, that's what we believe. If we knew, if we even had a reasonable suspicion, we could probably stop it. But —"

"But what has all this to do with me?" Page asked in perplexity.

"One possible source of leakage of information," Vance said, "is in my own house, or rather my aunt's house. She took me in as a small boy, and she has provided all the home I ever had."

"You don't think she —" Page began, horrified.

Cooper laughed. "You don't know Aunt Jane. She is a rock of integrity. The trouble is that she is one of those terribly plain-spoken women, and she speaks before she thinks. She might do so if she had the slightest suspicion. No, the situation is that she has taken a fancy to a young woman who claims to be her goddaughter. Now the girl has suggested that she pay a more or less indefinite visit to my aunt's house."

"Claims to be? Could there be any doubt about that?"

"Aunt Jane hasn't seen her goddaughter since she was five years old. She hasn't even a photograph of her."

"But can't you warn your aunt?"

"I repeat, you don't know Aunt Jane. She could no more

conceal her distrust than she could fly. And if she suspected anything was wrong, she would make no bones about getting rid of Beverly Main. That's my aunt's real weakness. She is a woman who cannot compromise, no matter what is at stake."

"But if you don't trust this girl and you can't warn your aunt, can't you at least move out temporarily? Go to a hotel or to your club?"

"And make clear to someone as to where my suspicions lie? Again no."

"Are you sure she's the one?"

"Frankly I don't believe she is the girl she claims to be, though that may have nothing to do with Markham Electronics. My aunt is well-to-do, and this girl may simply be looking for some easy pickings. On the other hand, she may be straight as a die and I am doing her a great injustice, but that is a chance we can't afford to take. We have people checking and double-checking her background, but we can't afford to wait for their reports. So that is where you come in."

Vance Cooper's expression was intent as he looked across the table at his dull companion, at the heavy mourning, at the lifeless face, the dark glasses, the ruthlessly pulled back hair. In spite of his dislike of fortune hunters, he couldn't altogether blame the man who had been reluctant to marry this girl.

The waiter removed soup plates, brought Columbia River salmon baked in a wonderful sauce, browned potatoes, asparagus hollandaise, and a covered dish of hot rolls.

"What I want of you, Miss Wilburn, is to have you return to New York with me and occupy that spare room of Aunt Jane's."

"I?" Page was bewildered, caught off base. "What on earth — but why would your aunt be willing to take in a complete stranger? It doesn't make sense. I should think that would be the surest way to arouse suspicion."

"I told you that Aunt Jane brought me up; she's all the family I have. I'm all she has. At least — well, that is her tragedy. In the back of her mind I suspect she has matrimonial designs for me; she generally has." He smiled suddenly, a smile that began in his eyes and then lighted his face.

It wasn't like Jerry's smile, which was more engaging in a way. Jerry had always known the effect of his smile on women. Page tried to prevent her mind from running automatically to Jerry. She forced it back to the man across from her, the man who was quite unconscious of his charm and made no attempt to use it for his own advantage. A very worried man in spite of his smile.

"In fact," Vance went on, "since I was twenty-three Aunt Jane has been dangling attractive girls before me." Unexpectedly he laughed outright. "Good lord, I sound as though I had been spurning these proud beauties. Of course, it isn't like that at all. Probably they wouldn't have looked at me in any case. It's just that I prefer making my own choice, making up my own mind."

Seeing the firm line of his jaw — Jerry's had been more rounded and gave him a gentler air — Page thought, "I'll bet you do. No one will ever be able to shove you around."

"Poor Aunt Jane. I suppose none of us learn much from experience or by our mistakes. Aunt Jane has — had — an only child, a daughter. She ruled her with an iron hand and didn't give her much scope to find out what kind of person she really was. Anyhow, she decided how she was to live her life, and I think she had a candidate all picked out for Marta to marry. The result, and I suppose only Aunt Jane was surprised, was that Marta left home one day and never came back."

"How awful! Doesn't anyone know what became of her?"

"If Aunt Jane knows she has never said so. She has never mentioned Marta since then."

"How old was your cousin when she ran away?"

"Eighteen."

"Your aunt sounds rather hard."

"In many ways she is a fine person. But she's — so terribly sure that she is right."

Vance dropped the painful subject abruptly. "Anyhow, this time I'm pretty sure from the symptoms that it is Beverly Main she has in mind for me. So — do go ahead and eat that salmon while it is hot; it's wonderful — so my idea is to call Aunt Jane, say I'm engaged to be married and that I'd like to bring my girl — you — home with me. The ostensible reasons would be that I want you two to become acquainted and that you'll be shopping in New York for your trousseau. And that, by the way, is to be part of the deal. A whole wardrobe, Markham said."

"Oh, no." Page's voice was flat. "That is simply out of the question."

"Why is it?" he asked, and for the first time she really saw him: an agreeable man to look at, certainly; good but not obtrusive manners; steady eyes that met hers levelly. For a moment she recalled the long, narrow blue eyes of Jerry Brooks and thrust away the memory. Jerry's eyes had always been laughing; these were unexpectedly sober.

"Well —"

"There would be no awkwardness," he assured her. "The only part of this I dislike is having to deceive Aunt Jane. But we'll clear it all up eventually, and then she will understand and forgive me. We'll have to see a bit of each other, of course; that will be expected. But not too much. This next month will be a frantically busy time for me. But a few nights a week we can do a theater or something of the sort. For the rest, you can shop to your heart's content. And probably Aunt Jane will want to entertain you a bit."

When Page remained silent he said, "You see, this is the best cover I could think of. It keeps Beverly out of the house while we complete our check and find out what friends she has, whom she sees, all that. About all you would have to do — and that's only when Aunt Jane is around — is to try to pretend you find me attractive." He gave her a disarming grin. "As I'm her fair-haired boy she's going to expect that, you know."

Page started to repeat her "no" and unexpectedly remembered Leslie saying of her father that he hadn't cheated himself, he had met every adventure and enjoyed it to the hilt, even when he got hurt. Well, this was an adventure, wasn't it? New York, theaters, fabulous clothes, and, back of it all, the reason for it all, a real and desperately urgent purpose: the welfare of her own country.

"I'll do it," she said impulsively.

He stretched his hand across the table and clasped hers. "Good girl."

The waiter brought sherbet and coffee and withdrew again. Page looked across the table to see, for the first time, that her imperturbable host was embarrassed.

"What is it, Mr. Cooper?"

"You had better start calling me Vance, hadn't you? And you are Page. All right?"

"All right, Vance. I still wonder what is wrong."

"Well, look here, Page, would you mind not wearing mourning? That is, it doesn't strike quite the right note of jubilation of the happily engaged, does it? That is —"

And Page found herself laughing. She wondered what Vance found so surprising about that. He was seeing the transformation in her face, the quick, unexpected flash of gaiety that curved the beautifully shaped lips. She wasn't quite as moth-eaten as she had appeared to be. Apparently there was some faint possibility that emotion might stir behind the dead face. Not, he assured himself, that he wanted to arouse it. Heaven forbid.

Behind him a cool, somewhat mocking voice drawled, "Oh, Page. Nice to see you again. You're looking well."

Page was aware that she had rarely looked worse in her life. She looked up. Her heart had not missed a beat. She answered with equal coolness, "Hello, Jerry! You're looking on top of the world yourself. I want you to know my fiancé, Vance Cooper. Jerome Brooks, Vance."

Vance got to his feet. The young man behind him was extremely good-looking, though his mouth was ominously weak. For a moment Jerry betrayed his surprise, even a kind of bewilderment, a disbelief. Then, slowly, a look of amusement crossed his face.

"You are a lucky man, Mr. Cooper."

Vance thanked him gravely. "I know just how lucky I am."

Only Page was aware of the undertone in his voice, knew the full meaning of the hollow phrase. Anger flicked along her veins. So Vance thought he was getting a poor bargain, did he? It might be good for that young man to learn a salutary lesson. Spurn proud beauties, did he? Though this was manifestly unfair, she let her anger churn.

"When did this happen?" Jerry asked. "You just slipped away, Page." His tone was reproachful. "I never knew until today that you were with the Markham people." He looked at Vance. "I suppose that's how you met."

"What are you doing these days?" Page asked, not sure how much Vance wanted to have explained.

"Nothing that would interest you now," Jerry said.

When she did not contradict him he nodded to them both and went out of the restaurant. After he had gone, Vance started to speak, refrained with an effort. Personally, he thought, he would enjoy kicking that conceited young fellow all the way to the bay and then dumping him in, but there was no point in saying so. The idea at the moment was to establish a calm, detached, impersonal relationship with the pale, dim girl across the table, not to arouse her indignation and her protective instincts for the handsome young weakling who had jilted her. Looking across the table, perhaps because of those concealing dark glasses, he failed to see the spark of challenge in her eyes.

But what Aunt Jane would think of his taste he could easily imagine. Poor Aunt Jane was certainly in for a shock.

THREE

THAT NIGHT Page walked restlessly up and down the furnished room in which she had lived for several months. For once she was not aware of its shabbiness, she did not resent its discomfort, she did not think of its loneliness. She was trying to sort out her thoughts and feelings. Part of her rebelled at the thought of going to New York in company with this strange young man, of being forced as a guest upon a no-doubt-unwilling hostess, and under false pretenses, too.

Part of her was excited, churned up with excitement, at the idea of the New York trip, of an unlimited shopping allowance, of evenings of theater and perhaps music. Adventure, indeed. And with a five-thousand-dollar bonus she might have time to look around for a more congenial job, even to take a trip somewhere, anywhere. Why, there wasn't anything she couldn't do if she set her heart on it!

For the first time since Jerry had so ruthlessly discarded her, like tossing surplus cargo off a ship, she was thinking of the future with interest and hope. All these months she had dreaded walking down the streets of San Francisco in case she should encounter him. She had not been able to go away because she had no money except for her salary. She had avoided most of her old friends, afraid that they would speak of Jerry, perhaps even sympathize with her, the bitter kind of sympathy doled out to the women who cannot hold their men, the women who have nothing but their father's money with which to attract a man.

Never self-conscious as a girl, she had become more and more diffident, less and less sure of herself, unable to believe that she had any qualities to make a man love her.

And now, after all, she had met Jerry without pain or embarrassment; for the first time she had been at ease, more self-assured than he. She had seen the way he had summed up Vance Cooper. There had been a curious look of amusement on his face, as though he knew something to Vance's discredit, which was unlikely. At least she had no reason to feel apologetic about the man who had ostensibly become her fiancé. He had quite obviously dismissed Jerry as a negligible factor, and she was obscurely pleased. Now she need no longer fear encountering him. That, at least, was over. She was free of Jerry forever.

I know just how lucky I am, Vance had said.

Tomorrow, Page decided, I'll go to the best place in San Francisco and have my hair cut and styled. After all, she explained carefully to herself, I don't want to make a bad impression on Vance's Aunt Jane. Not that I care in the least what he thinks of me; still, Mr. Markham would want me to carry this thing off in a convincing manner. She found her lips curving in an amused smile. You watch out, Mr. Vance Cooper. You are going to get the surprise of your life!

She was smiling when she fell asleep, smiling when she awakened in the morning from the best night's sleep she had had in months. Even the lumpy studio couch could not disturb her rest. No bad dreams, no tossing on the pillow, no feeling of humiliation or defeat. Life, here I come! she told herself gaily.

Because it was Saturday she slept late. It was nearly noon when she returned from the beauty parlor. Her hair, soft, lustrous, gleaming like pale honey, hung loosely, waving on her neck. The dark glasses had been tossed into the wastebasket. Her eyes were a deep dark blue, fringed with improbably long lashes, her cheeks glowed with excitement. Her lips were deep red, and now one could see how beautifully shaped they were.

There was a tap at the door and her landlady, wheezing from the stairs, handed her a big box. "Came for you this morning, Miss Wilburn. I signed for it."

Page, aware that the woman would not have bothered to bring up the box if she had not been consumed with curiosity about its contents, said merely, "Thank you. That was very kind."

The landlady settled herself comfortably in the doorway, prepared to wait. Obviously she did not intend to go until her curiosity had been satisfied. She stared at Page in amazement. "My, I'd hardly have recognized you! With your hair fixed like that and without those dark glasses you're one of the prettiest girls I ever saw. I'd never have guessed it," she added naïvely.

Page laughed. "Thank you," she said again. She made no move to open the box.

"I was wondering — well," as Page appeared to have forgotten the interesting box, "I figured you might be getting some new clothes, and that's the most expensive shop in town. My daughter-in-law got a dress there once, and what she paid for it — scandalous it was! I told my son right then and there —"

"Don't let me keep you," Page said. "I know you must have a lot to do."

"You kept me busy this morning and that's a fact. So I was wondering —"

"I did?" Page was surprised.

"Telephone. Must have had half a dozen calls. Up and down stairs. Up and down stairs. That's how I've spent the morning."

"I'm so sorry you were bothered. Was there any message?"

"No, just asked for you and when you'd be back."

Leslie, of course.

"Where you had gone and if you was alone. Things like that."

Then definitely not Leslie who would not dream of prying.

As Page showed no indication of providing any information, the landlady sighed heavily and went out, closing the door reluctantly behind her.

As soon as she had gone, Page ran to her little kitchenette for a knife to cut the cord and open the big box. Somewhat to her surprise, she noticed that the seals had been broken, which was strangely careless for a shop of so high a reputation. This, of course, must be the present Leslie Trevor had insisted on giving her. She opened the cardboard cover and gasped. Under the thin layer of tissue paper the dress was an exquisite sheath of gray as filmy as smoke, with a wool coat of a darker shade. There were long, soft kid gloves of jade-green, jade shoes, a tiny jade hat and handbag.

There was also a package in the corner, wrapped in layer upon layer of tissue paper. Page removed the wrappings and stared in disbelief. In her hand she held a jade pendant, a carved figurine that was hung on an unexpectedly heavy chain. It was, she thought, the loveliest thing she had ever seen, but it was too much; she couldn't let Leslie do this for her. The clothes were one thing; this magnificent work of art was too much. Just because she had said that she loved jade. Her fingers stroked the pendant softly, delighting in the exquisite texture.

She would have to return it. Then she remembered Leslie's words: Stingy receiver.

She removed the heavy mourning and dressed in the light, smoky-gray sheath, hung the pendant around her neck, put on the wool coat, slipped on the jade slippers, adjusted the tiny hat on her honey-colored hair, gathered up handbag and gloves.

For a long time she looked at the glowing girl in the mirror. This was what she had been like before Jerry jilted her. She had almost forgotten.

"Miss Wilburn!" the landlady bawled from the foot of the stairs. "Telephone."

Page ran down the stairs. As she closed the door of the telephone booth in the lower hall firmly behind her she saw her landlady's startled eyes as she summed up the change in her appearance.

The cool, mocking voice, to her stunned surprise, was that of Jerry Brooks. He said lightly, "This is Jerry. Forgotten me?"

"Just about," she admitted.

There was a brief silence as though he were taken aback. Then he said, the old caressing note in his voice, "Page, my sweet, don't be angry."

"I'm not," she assured him.

"I've called several times this morning. Where on earth were you?"

"Out."

"How about lunch?"

"I'm lunching with Vance," she lied blandly.

"Vance? Oh, your new boyfriend."

"That's right."

"Known him long?" he asked casually.

"That hardly concerns you, does it, Jerry?"

"Everything about you concerns me. Look here, darling, I'm afraid you never quite understood. You know how I love you, how I always have, but I've been committed to a diplomatic career ever since prep school days; my parents have their hearts set on it."

"You're wrong, Jerry. I understand perfectly, and I hope the next girl will have plenty of money to support you in your career. Knowing you, I doubt if you would make the same mistake twice."

"Page — Page, please wait — please listen —" There was something genuine, something almost frantic in his voice as she set down the telephone quietly.

She had opened the door of the booth when the telephone rang again. For a moment she hesitated, but it was unlikely that Jerry would have had time to dial the number again, even if he had wanted to call back in the face of her rebuff.

"May I speak to Miss Wilburn, please? . . . Oh, Page, this is Vance Cooper. Something seems to have cropped up in New York that is going to rush things a bit. Can you possibly be ready to leave in the morning? I ought to be there tomorrow evening for an important meeting. I didn't intend to stampede you into a decision like this but matters seem to have got a bit out of control."

"Of course I can be ready. The only trouble is that I have no wardrobe that isn't mourning."

"We can remedy that in New York. Aunt Jane will understand that I practically dragged you onto the plane without giving you time to pack."

Aunt Jane, Page reflected, appeared to be a very understanding woman, which was not the picture Vance had given of her in the first place. Well, all she could do was to hope for the best.

Vance concluded arrangements hurriedly, gave her the number and time of the flight and planned to meet her at the airport.

"And you had better take down Aunt Jane's address, in case you want your mail forwarded."

Not having a pencil and paper at hand, Page repeated the instructions aloud so as to fix them in her memory.

"Bad news, dear?" the landlady asked, studying Page's new clothes with avid eyes, her eyes raking the face that had been so expressionless and that now was vivid and alive. "I thought I heard something about a plane. You planning to go somewhere?"

Knowing that the landlady had heard every word, Page said quietly, "I'm leaving for New York in the morning."

"How about your room? You've paid me up through next week, but you can't hardly expect me to hold it long after that unless I'm sure you'll be back. A lovely room like that. Lots of people looking for a comfortable, quiet room in a well-run place these days."

"I'll let you know about my plans in plenty of time so you won't lose a week's rent," Page assured her.

In her room she dragged a battered suitcase out of the closet and went through her scanty wardrobe. It was in even worse shape than she had expected. The few dresses she had kept from the happy days were hopelessly out of date, the wrong length, the wrong lines. She couldn't face the formidable Aunt Jane in these. She would simply have to go with the one gray outfit and start shopping on Monday morning. The speed with which things were happening took her breath away.

She hunted out her address book, tucked it into her new handbag, and then made a list of minor things she must buy before the flight.

Then, with a look at her watch, she ran down the stairs again. She would have time only for a drugstore sandwich if she were to finish all the errands she had listed. But first she must thank Leslie for her wonderful present and tell her about her plans for the immediate future.

The maid who answered the telephone was sorry. Mrs. Trevor had gone to see her mother-in-law who was seriously ill and she was not expected back before tomorrow evening. Yes, the maid would take a message. Miss Wilburn was leaving for New York tomorrow morning. She could be reached in care of Mrs. Thomas Wentley at 600 East Thirty-sixth Street, New York, until further notice. And Miss Wilburn was overwhelmed by the — what was that word? — munificent present.

Feeling a little downcast because she could not thank Leslie in person or tell her about the exciting events in which she was becoming involved, Page went into the crisp October air. Leslie had been right. There was something about the sight of the gay color of the jade-green gloves and the green handbag that lifted her heart. There was something, too, in the eyes that followed her that built her morale. More than one man turned for a second look at the slim radiant girl with the honey-colored hair and the dark blue eyes.

Mentally recalling her shopping list, Page thought: Drugstore first. I'll have a sandwich and then pick up the odds and ends I need there. Better leave the heavy packages until last. Then I'll take a taxi home. With a five-thousand-dollar bonus in the offing, as well as a month's salary, she could afford to take taxis once more.

The high heels of her jade slippers tapped briskly along the street, unlike the flat black shoes with rubber heels that she had worn so long. And when she became aware of the sound of her own swiftly tapping feet she heard other footsteps that seemed to keep pace with her own. Which, of course, was nonsense.

As it was long past the usual lunch time, there were only a few schoolgirls giggling at the counter while they drank ice cream sodas. Page ordered a sandwich, and while she waited for it she looked at the revolving stand that displayed paperback books. She gave the stand a swifter whirl than she had intended, and a woman who was reaching for a book turned a startled face toward her. Then her eyes dropped from Page's face to the jade figurine that glowed against the gray dress.

Page frowned, wondering where she had seen the woman before, a fat woman in a shabby brown coat. Oh, of course, she had been looking at Gump's window when Page and Leslie had stopped there.

"Sorry," Page said, "I didn't realize anyone else was looking at the books."

"More of them every day, aren't there?" the woman said, nodding at the revolving shelves. "A real miracle the way they keep being published."

Page nodded and devoted her attention to the sandwich.

The woman was still deciding which book she wanted when Page left the drugstore, after checking off the items she had bought there.

When she had scratched off the last one on her list she sighed with relief because her arms were filled with packages; she couldn't carry another thing. She was about to look around for a cruising taxi when she stopped short. Vance's Aunt Jane! What on earth could she take to Vance's Aunt Jane, when she knew nothing whatever of her tastes? Someone bumped into her, a tall man, wide-shouldered and slim-hipped, with a bronzed face and a ten-gallon cowboy hat.

"Ooops, sorry!" he said, steadying her.

"It was my fault. I was thinking."

"It takes you that way, does it?" he said, grinning, and Page laughed with him.

"How do I get to Chinatown?" the man asked. "My wife likes me to bring her something special from every place I visit on business trips and I thought —"

"Of course, Chinatown is San Francisco's special thing," Page said. She indicated the way and then thought, "It's only a few blocks. I'll get something from Chinatown for Aunt Jane!" She rearranged her packages and started in the direction she had given the big friendly man from the wide-open spaces.

As she reached the famous Chinese section she began to look in windows. Chinese silks? But she didn't know what colors would be suitable. Jade? No, she couldn't afford jade, and, anyhow, her hostess gift should be something simple and unpretentious.

She walked on, unaware of the gradual fading of the light from the sky as it was replaced by the lights of China-

town. There was a dark, narrow alley between two buildings. When Page passed it, a hand reached out, snatched at
the jade pendant and tugged. Page screamed, a second hand
came over her mouth and she was dragged back into the alley, away from the safety of the lighted street with its
crowds of people.

She dropped her packages, tugging at the hand with all
her strength, managed to free her mouth long enough to
draw a long breath and scream. Then she was falling back-
ward, there was a scuffling, the sound of blows, and a woman's loud cry that was not hers.

"What's going on here?"

That was a policeman, helping her to her feet. She could
hear the sound of thudding feet in the alley. A woman said
in excitement, "We saw someone grab her. My husband
tried to stop him."

The policeman looked Page over for signs of damage
while he listened to the young couple who had intervened
and saved her.

"He got away," the man said in disgust. "I thought I
was pretty good but he ran like an Olympic star."

"Did you get a good look at him, miss?"

Page shook her head. "Just that hand grabbing my pendant and the one over my mouth. He couldn't take the pendant because the chain is too strong to break."

"Nothing at all to tell you what he looked like?"

Again she shook her head, dabbed at a drop of blood on
her lip. "He was strong, and he wore a ring on his left
hand. It cut my lip."

The policeman went down the alley, came back to say
there was no sign of the man. There were a hundred different holes he could have bolted into. Laboriously he took

their statements, while the helpful young man picked up her scattered packages.

"Sure you are all right?" the policeman asked Page. "You don't want to see a doctor?"

"I'd like a taxi," she said, her voice shaking, aware that her legs were unsteady.

The obliging policeman called a cab and, after thanking the young couple who had come to her rescue, Page was driven home.

Once safely in her room she saw the small cut on her lip where the man's hand had crushed her mouth. At least her heart was steady now, her breathing was normal, her legs no longer felt like cooked macaroni.

When she had prepared and eaten a light supper and cleaned up everything so there would be no food in the refrigerator to spoil after she left, she began to pace the room. Odd how that incident had upset her. She was unhurt; the jade figurine was safe. Nonetheless, she had to admit that she had been frightened, more badly frightened than was reasonable. There had been something menacing about that invisible man with the strong hands who had jerked her toward the alley. What would have happened to her if the young couple had not been the kind who feel responsible for their fellow human beings? Would he have been content just to steal the jade or would he have — hurt her?

She switched out the light and for a long time stood at the window looking out. What would happen before she saw San Francisco again? The day that had begun so brightly had ended in fog. Fog turned streetlights into dim globes seen through mist. People on the street were as vague as shadows. A dim shape across the street moved, and the movement caught her eyes. Even through the fog she felt that there was something familiar about the woman, about the cumbersome way in which she walked. For heaven's sake, Page thought in disgust, I'm getting too darned imaginative. I seem to be haunted by fat women in brown coats.

The woman crossed the street, vanished under the entrance to Page's building. Someone was coming quietly up the stairs. In a sudden panic, Page ran to shove home the bolt on her door. A moment later she felt the handle turn under her hand. Turn again. She hardly breathed until she felt a floorboard move under her foot, and then the stairs creaked as someone went down.

She slipped back to her darkened window. After a long time she saw the heavy woman come out of the building and cross the street. When Page finally got into bed, a chair securely hooked under the doorknob, the woman was still standing there, looking up at the window.

FOUR

VANCE was standing at a newsstand buying a paper when Page arrived at the airport.

"Good morning, Vance," she said cheerfully, and he turned to face her.

"Good morning." He touched his hat, looked at her in puzzled half-recognition, then in shock. Good lord, the girl was lovely, with eyes like deep pools, with — she was actually making him feel poetic. But who was she? He hadn't met any girl as attractive as this more than half a dozen times in his life. Then how could he have forgotten her? And she knew him well enough to call him Vance.

If you can forget a girl who looks like this, you are slipping, he told himself.

She laughed, her momentary shyness evaporating like mist in a hot sun before the admiration in his eyes. "It's customary to recognize your fiancée when you meet her." Mischief danced in the blue eyes with their long lashes.

"Page!" he exclaimed. He thought in consternation, I wasn't prepared for anything like this. What has happened to the girl? Why she's a beauty. Aloud he said, trying to sound casual, "What about some coffee? There's plenty of time."

"Thank you. I overslept and didn't bother with breakfast."

"This way, then." He led her toward the lunchroom.

"Won't you have something more: toast, eggs, grapefruit?"

She shook her head. "I'm much too excited to eat."

When the coffee had been set before them a man called, "Vance!"

Heads turned in response to that loud, cheery voice. At the far end of the counter sat a big man with a bronzed face.

"Miles!" Vance said, and the big man got up, strode toward them, and held out his hand.

"Well, howdy, stranger." His eyes traveled on to Page, stopped in startled recognition.

"Page," Vance said, "this is Miles Forrest, the best tackle we had when I was at Dartmouth. My fiancée, Page Wilburn."

Miles crushed Page's hand in his big one. "Well, what do you know? Running into you again like this."

"Again?" Vance looked from one to the other in surprise. "You've met before?"

"Head-on," the westerner said, and laughed. "You know what a clumsy ox I am. I nearly mowed down the little lady in Chinatown yesterday." He beamed at Page. "Beautiful thing," he said and she was startled until she realized that he was referring not to her but to the jade figurine. "I picked up a gift for my wife in Chinatown. That's quite a place, isn't it? Not much like the old days with the dope and the smuggling and the crime. You wouldn't remember," he smiled at Page, "the old stories about the mysterious and inscrutable Chinese and the wild things that went on down there."

"They still go on," Page told him. "Just after I met you I ran head-on into some real trouble."

"You did? What happened?" Miles asked.

A loudspeaker announced their flight; Vance said, "See

you in New York," and led Page to the plane. The big man waved to them cheerfully.

"Real westerner, isn't he?" she said. "He's more like something in a western movie than in real life. All he needs is a couple of six-shooters."

Vance laughed. "That is typical of Miles. Something in him never seems to grow up. Whenever he comes West he likes to dress the part, everything but the six-shooters. Wait until you see him in New York, and you will because he's not only a colleague but a great friend of mine. White tie and tails and clothes made by an English tailor."

She shook her head, baffled. "No one would guess it," she admitted. "But I can believe he was a wonderful football tackle."

"He is also," Vance said, "one of the most brilliant electronics engineers at Markham."

She laughed. "How does he dress for that? In a space suit?"

Vance chuckled. "He probably would if he could get away with it."

When Page was settled by the window with Vance beside her she looked around at the other passengers. She drew a quick breath and instinctively groped for Vance's hand. It closed warmly and comfortingly over hers.

"What's wrong?" he asked gently. "Your first jet flight?"

"Yes, but it's not that. It's — Jerry. He just got on the plane. See, the third row ahead on the right?"

"Is that the young man I met at lunch?"

She nodded. The gaiety that had warmed her face was draining out. His hand tightened over hers.

"Look here, Page, you are engaged to me. Remember?

That conceited puppy has nothing to do with you." He was surprised by the degree of feeling in his voice.

She gave him a quick look. "So you know about — Jerry and me."

"Well, Markham just mentioned it."

She tugged at her hand, the color deepening in her face. His grasp tightened. As the jet took off she clutched at him, grateful for his nearness, for the safety he represented.

Long after the seatbelts were unfastened she discovered that he was still holding her hand. This time, when she tugged at it, he released it promptly. Without giving her time to speak, he began to tell her about the country over which they were flying, pointing out mountains and rivers and cities and lonely farms and forests.

"We've conquered all that by sheer guts," he said. "We have given man the best life known anywhere on earth."

"And yet people seem to resent us for it. Our material civilization, they call it with a sneer."

He grinned at her. "So they do. But as soon as they get a tenth of what we have they proudly call it progress."

"The days of building must have been wonderful," she said, her face glowing.

He looked at her enchanting profile. One thing sure, Aunt Jane would not wonder why he had chosen this girl. She would probably wonder how he had ever had the luck to find and win her.

"We are still building, Page. We'll always be building. And it's just as wonderful. Of course, even here, there are people who try to tear down. That's easy for any fool or neurotic to do. The difficult thing is to build, a lot more difficult than tearing down."

"But not as adventurous now as in the old days," she said regretfully.

"There is plenty of adventure," he assured her, "and plenty of danger. And, by the way, speaking of danger, what did you mean about running head-on into something in Chinatown?"

When Page had told him, he leaned closer. "Yes, I can see a tiny cut on your lip. But, good heavens, Page, you should be more careful!"

She began to laugh and, reluctantly, he joined her. Then he sobered.

"You weren't hurt at all?"

"Except for shock and fright; I'm just not the heroine type, Vance. I learned that. Heroines always seem to rise to the occasion, to be ready to risk anything —"

"Then they are very foolish," he commented.

"Well, I didn't. I was simply petrified," she said frankly.

"Why?"

"I don't know. A kind of feeling — or perhaps I'm getting too imaginative."

"It was that jade figurine he snatched at, you say?"

Page nodded. "But the chain is so strong he couldn't break it."

Vance studied the figurine, fingered the chain. "That's queer," he said. "A beautiful thing like that hung on a steel chain! No wonder the thief couldn't break it." He examined the pendant. "That is exquisite work. It must be hundreds of years old. Is it a family heirloom?"

She shook her head and for a moment the bitter curve was back on the warm lips. "All the family heirlooms and jewelry and *objets d'art* were sold to pay the bills after my father died. No, this was given me by a friend, a very dear friend."

"Who was he?" Vance sounded rather snappish, Page thought, and she looked at him in surprise. Then her eyes widened and she bit her lip to hide her smile. Vance was jealous.

"Leslie Trevor, my oldest friend. She is the one who provided this outfit so that I'd get out of mourning."

"It's — very becoming," he said lamely, but Page did not seem to be disappointed by his lack of enthusiasm. She remembered his face when he had caught sight of her at the airport. He had been completedly bowled over, though he had made a quick recovery. Apparently Mr. Vance Cooper was not a young man to be swept off his feet without a struggle.

After a pause he asked, "What did you mean about being too imaginative?"

She told him then about the two people whose reflections she had seen in Gump's window, and how she kept imagining that she saw them again: the ferret-faced man in the restaurant where she had lunched with Vance, and the fat woman in brown at the drugstore where she had lunched alone yesterday and again last night outside her building, and her conviction that the woman had tried to get into her room, that she had kept watch outside for a long time.

"That's odd," he said thoughtfully, but he did not seem to be amused, nor did he dismiss it as lightly as she had expected. "You never had this feeling of being — watched before, did you?"

"Why no," she said in a tone of surprise.

"At the moment, Page," he said soberly, "I'm a dangerous person to know. If I had suspected for a moment that you would be involved in anything, that I would be bringing you any trouble —"

"You think," her voice dropped to a whisper, "this might have something to do with Operation Homebase? I don't see how it possibly could. I saw them both before we lunched together, before any connection could be made between us."

"I agree that it doesn't seem very probable. And no one would possibly believe you could get possession of information that would have any value. But be very careful, will you? If anything arouses your suspicion, tell me at once. Promise me that."

"I promise," Page said fervently. "If you had any idea what a coward I am —"

"You, Page?" said a light, mocking voice. The man who had been sitting beside Vance had gone to the washroom and Jerry, who apparently had been awaiting such an opportunity, had slipped into his seat.

"Oh, hello, Jerry. I thought I saw you up there. Going to New York?"

"Going your way, Page darling." Jerry glanced, half impudently, half challengingly, at Vance. "I saw her first, you know."

Vance returned the look but made no comment. Page flushed with anger.

As the silence was awkwardly prolonged, and neither Page nor Vance made the slightest attempt to break it, Jerry asked, "Did you two meet at the Markham Company?" He looked at Vance. "I understand that you are an employee of theirs too." His tone indicated that Vance was probably a night watchman. He was deliberately insolent, but Vance did not rise to the bait. He returned Jerry's mocking look, and it was Jerry whose eyes shifted away first.

He turned to Page. "You just — dropped out of sight, darling," he said reproachfully.

"I did, didn't I?" She looked past him to the passenger who was waiting for his seat.

Jerry got up. "See you soon, Pet," he said to Page, nodded curtly to Vance, and went back to his own seat.

"Now what was all that in aid of?" Vance wondered aloud.

Page was furious. It had been bad enough for Jerry to jilt her cold-bloodedly, but for him to assume now that he had only to get that caressing note in his voice, only to smile, and she would fall into his arms, was too much. As though she had no pride, no self-respect. As though, she found herself thinking in profound surprise, she were not with a man who was worth ten Jerrys.

"He was terribly rude to you," she told Vance. "I apologize for him."

"Rude on purpose," he said. "That's what interested me."

"And you just — took it." She could not keep the disappointment and reproach out of her voice.

He smiled broadly. "What interests me is why this deliberate attempt to start a quarrel with me. I wouldn't have said that was his line at all."

"What would you say was his line?"

"Letting other people take the jumps for him," he replied, and then thought that he had made a mistake. However, he could detect no resentment in Page's expression.

"Tell me about your Aunt Jane," she said, dismissing

Jerry from her thoughts. "Does she know that I am coming with you?"

"Oh, yes, of course. I called her yesterday after I had talked to you, said I had met the one and only girl, and that I was so afraid of losing her that I was practically dragging her off to New York by the hair so she wouldn't be out of my sight until we were married. I wasn't taking any chances."

"That," Page commented, laughing, "was a bit extreme, wasn't it? Surely your aunt isn't going to believe any such nonsense as that. Was she much — upset?" When Vance hesitated, she said, "You might as well tell me. If she is as direct a person as you've described, I'll know the moment I meet her how she feels about me. It would help to be prepared."

"Well, she was taken aback, of course. But, being Aunt Jane, she told me how happy she was for me, how she looked forward to knowing you, to welcoming you into the family."

He was, Page thought, speaking too carefully — probably editing what had been his aunt's consternation and disappointment. She said only, "How gracious of her."

"She's a gracious person. I think you are going to like her. I hope you will. If you can get through that rather formidable barrier she sets up, you will find that she is pure gold. And you can do it if anyone could." He cleared his throat, went on hastily. "What bothers her is simply that Beverly Main asked to stay with her for a few weeks; but Aunt Jane told me she would arrange something, perhaps suggest that Beverly postpone her visit."

After a moment Page said tentatively, "Vance?"

"Yes, darl — yes, Page?" Watch it, you fool, he warned himself savagely. This engagement isn't for real.

"It was Beverly who suggested visiting your aunt, not your aunt who asked her?"

"Yes, it was Beverly. Look here, Page, Beverly Main is as smart as they come and quick as a flash. Watch your step when you talk with her in case she sets any traps. That is, if you ever have to meet, though I hope I've forestalled her coming. Be careful what you say about how long we've known each other, how we met, our plans for the future, all that."

"All right," she agreed, "but in that case we had better make sure that our stories match."

"Well, let's see. I heard a fire engine, raced up the ladder into the burning building and dragged you out at the risk of my life. Naturally you were impressed by my heroism."

"Not all that impressed. Anyhow, that's old stuff. Instead of a ladder, I let down my hair like Rapunzel and you climbed up to save me."

"Probably good scalp treatment but that's doing it the hard way. No, we can do better than that. A mine caved in and I tunneled my way through and saved you at the eleventh hour."

"What was I doing in a mine?"

"That," he told her, "was your own business. Naturally I wasn't vulgar enough to inquire."

"Naturally."

An hour later, Page sat back, flushed with laughter. From one wild and irresponsible suggestion to another they had carried their nonsense. All restraint was gone. All sense of strangeness between them had dissolved. Laughter is a wonderful bridge to understanding.

"Look." He touched her arm. "The lights of New York."

Page looked out on one of the world's most wonderful sights, the towers of New York thrusting into the sky, ablaze with light; Manhattan between its two dark rivers, linked to the mainland by bridge after gleaming bridge; the streaks of light that were cars as small as ants moving over the hundreds of miles of city roads.

She watched in mounting excitement. Down there were the theaters and the art galleries, great music and great universities, the hub of the world's business and science, people engaged in every conceivable occupation, apartments of fantastic luxury and grim slums, the UN to hold the line of peace and men plotting to overthrow the government, people who were helping to build a better world and criminals who were preparing to destroy it. Ambition and hope, dreams and despair, activity of every conceivable kind, emotion on every level. New York!

Page's heart thudded, her breath came fast. Leslie couldn't say she was turning her back on life now. She was running headlong to meet it.

FIVE

SOMEWHAT to Page's surprise, Vance directed his taxi driver to take them to the Plaza.

"Aunt Jane told me she had an engagement for dinner so long-standing that she could not possibly break it," he explained. "We'll dine at the Plaza and then go on to the house later."

Halfway through dinner, he stopped in the middle of an amusing story to say accusingly, "You haven't heard a single word I've been saying."

"I really begin to think I am haunted." Page shook her head so that the soft honey-colored waves brushed her neck.

"Don't tell me," Vance laughed, "that you've seen the fat woman in brown again."

"No, but Old Rat Eyes is just four tables away — no, more to your left and a little back of you."

Vance dropped his cigarette case, bent over to retrieve it, glanced carelessly around.

"The thin fellow in the suit with the green stripes?"

Page nodded, careful not to glance at the man again.

"Are you sure about that?"

"If it isn't the same man it is his twin brother." There was no mistaking the absolute conviction in her voice. "But — why, Vance, why?"

"When did this start?"

Page thought for a moment. "It was the day Mr. Markham called me to his office. That day I had lunch with my friend, Mrs. Gordon Trevor." Her hand touched the jade figurine. "She is the one who gave me this, as I explained to you."

"Tell me what happened."

"Nothing happened. By chance we passed Gump's and naturally we stopped to look in the windows. I saw the man and the fat woman in brown — at least, their reflections, you know."

"Can you remember what you and your friend were talking about? What was said? Was there any reference to the Markham Company?"

Page thought about it, shook her head doubtfully. Leslie had accused her of wearing mourning for Jerry, and she had denied it. For some reason she did not care to discuss that with Vance.

"Leslie said I was turning my back on life, that I had packed it away in mothballs." She laughed ruefully. "She asked me to let her give me one outfit of clothes with some bright color, at least as accessories." Page raised her hand, dropped it helplessly. "There wasn't anything, honestly, Vance."

"Think hard. Try to imagine that you are standing outside Gump's window." Something in his urgency made Page attempt to visualize the scene. "Actual words if you possibly can," he said, still in that urgent way.

"But that was all there was. Oh, I talked about jade. Looking in Gump's made me think of it, of course. I said it was really the miracle stone. People could have all the diamonds in the world, but I would take jade. That's when Leslie suggested jade-green for my accessories."

"I'm honestly sorry to hound you this way." Vance was contrite. "But I keep hoping that somewhere I'll find a lead."

"And you haven't found one?"

"Frankly, no." Then he sat staring at her.

"What's wrong? Soot on my nose?"

"Jade," he said frowning. "It's the only possible tie-up that I can see."

"But why —"

"Someone tried to snatch that jade pendant you are wearing," he reminded her.

"Oh, really, Vance!"

"I know it sounds absurd. It doesn't make any sense to me either. How would anyone know your friend Mrs. Trevor would send you a gift of such great value?"

"That's queer." Page's voice rose in excitement and then dropped low at the alarmed look on Vance's face. It was an odd feeling to know that they were observed, perhaps overheard. "I just remembered. The jade pendant was in the box in which these clothes came."

"Well?"

"The seals on the box were broken. I remember thinking at the time how careless it was to send anything valuable in that condition."

"So someone could have put the pendant into the box after it was delivered at your house. Someone wanted to be sure it was in your possession. But — would that be possible?"

Page thought, her brow furrowing. Then she nodded. "I think so, yes. My landlady signs for packages and then just leaves them on a table downstairs. The outside door is always unlocked, until midnight, that is. Anyone could go in without being noticed. The only reason she brought the box up to me herself was because she was dying of curiosity to know what I had bought at such an expensive store."

"So someone could have smuggled the pendant to you by breaking the seals on the box addressed to you and slipping it in; someone else tried to snatch it away."

"But the one who tried to steal it in Chinatown must have been an ordinary thief who had nothing to do with this other business."

"Do you think so, Page? I have the queerest hunch that someone has had an eye on you all the time."

"And that someone has an eye on me now," she said, her voice a trifle unsteady.

"I'll have my eye on you, too," Vance reminded her. He started to say that Markham was watching her as well, but decided it would be better not to. It might frighten her. Aware that she was keyed up from her near accident of the day before in Chinatown, her first jet flight, the approaching ordeal of meeting his aunt, he allowed the talk to drift aimlessly. He spoke idly of New York traffic regulations, hoped that it was not too late in the season for her to see the brilliant autumn foliage in New England. He would try to manage a free weekend for an excursion to Vermont and New Hampshire. He pointed out several celebrities in the restaurant, but he was careful not to look again in the direction of the man with the weasel face.

By the time their taxi drew up before the little four-story house on East Thirty-sixth Street in the Murray Hill section of New York, he was relieved to see that her tension had relaxed. He had spent most of the taxi trip looking over his shoulder but, if they were being tailed, he saw no evidence of it.

This would have pleased the weasel-faced man who had

had the foresight to precede and not to follow them, and who was waiting, crouched on the steps leading down to the areaway of the old brownstone house when they climbed the stairs to the front door.

"My aunt owns the first two floors," Vance was explaining. "The two upper stories are occupied by a Hollywood scriptwriter who spends only a few months a year in New York, so that it is really like having a private house."

The door was opened by a middle-aged man in a white jacket, whose face lighted up when he saw Vance.

"It's good to see you back, Mr. Cooper." He looked at Page with the frank curiosity of a man who had long been with the family. "And I suppose this is your young lady."

"Got it in one, Perkins! This is my girl."

"Well, I always knew you'd pick a winner."

"Is my aunt in?"

"Mrs. Wentley just came home. She is in her upstairs sitting room. She said to be sure to send you up right away, and would you and the young lady be wanting any coffee?"

Vance glanced at Page, who shook her head.

"No, thanks." Vance had Page precede him from the narrow outside corridor into a formal drawing room out of which a white circular staircase wound its way up to the second floor.

In spite of Vance's comments, Page had built an imaginary picture in her mind of his Aunt Jane. Mrs. Wentley would be dainty and old-fashioned and white-haired, with perhaps just a touch of the steel of Whistler's mother. So when a tall woman, built on large lines, with dark hair only lightly dusted with gray and a regal carriage came forward to meet her she was taken aback.

"Aunt Jane," Vance said, "this is my girl, Page Wilburn."

The tall woman looked down at the girl who stood beside Vance, summed her up in one clear glance from head to foot, and held out both hands.

"Welcome home, my dear," she said warmly. "Because Vance's home is yours, of course."

"That is very kind of you, Mrs. Wentley."

"Kind. Nonsense." The tall woman turned to kiss her nephew. She was nearly as tall as he and more heavily built. She carried with her an air of authority that could afford to be unstressed because it was not often challenged. "How clever of you, Vance, to win a girl like this."

He hugged his aunt, and Page was aware of the strong bond of affection and trust between them. "I'm a very clever guy," he assured her.

And a girl laughed.

Vance, the smile gone from his face, released his aunt. Page was aware of a kind of stiffness, then he seemed to be relaxed, smiling. He turned to the girl who was coming, unannounced, up the circular staircase.

"Hello, Beverly," he said coolly. "This is a pleasant surprise."

"Is it?"

Her extreme slenderness was emphasized by the clothes she wore, by her excessively short skirt. She had a high-cheekboned face like a model's. Her eyes and mouth were heavily made up. She had a husky voice and a sullen, full-lipped mouth.

Without the extreme clothes she would have been an unusually attractive girl. With them she was exotic rather than charming, an effect she undoubtedly sought deliberately. Her eyes traveled insolently over Page, turned to Mrs. Wentley.

"Dear Mrs. Wentley," she gushed, "I'm so sorry to be late. As I wrote you, I expected to be here hours ago."

"My dear," Mrs. Wentley said, sounding rather at a loss, "I am so sorry. There appears to have been a mistake. Didn't you get my telegram?"

"Telegram? No." Beverly tossed off her jacket without waiting to be asked and seated herself, thoroughly at home in the charming, informal sitting room. She drew a package of cigarettes out of her handbag, waited for Vance to give her a light, looking up at him while she did so. It was a look that demanded his attention but Vance, busying himself with the lighter, did not appear to notice it.

"What a pity!" Mrs. Wentley exclaimed. "I sent you a message saying that Vance was bringing home his fiancée and that I wouldn't have a room free for some time. I suggested that you postpone your visit at least until after Thanksgiving."

"No, I didn't get it. And I didn't know Vance was going to marry anyone. He certainly," and spite showed in her voice, "doesn't act like an engaged man."

Not being a fool, the girl saw the instant distaste in Mrs. Wentley's face. Her mouth drooped disconsolately. "Vance never told me. I suppose now I'll just be in the way; you won't want me here."

She was certainly, Page thought, trying to make things as awkward as possible.

"There is no reason, since you are here, why you shouldn't enjoy a New York visit," Mrs. Wentley said. "I'll call the Beekman Towers. You'd have a stupendous view from there."

"Well, I'm afraid I couldn't afford it. Somehow I just assumed I was going to have Marta's room —"

There was a frozen silence. Then Mrs. Wentley said, "I'd expect you to be my guest there as well as here, my dear." Without waiting for any further comment, she picked up the telephone beside her chair, checked a small directory, and dialed a number.

"This is Mrs. Thomas Wentley . . . a room with a view for a young friend of mine, Miss Beverly Main. My guest, of course . . . Yes, naturally, meals whenever she wants to have them there . . . Tonight. Oh," her eyes rested vaguely on Beverly who had made herself very comfortable and seemed prepared to spend the rest of the evening, "within the next half hour . . . Thank you."

She put down the telephone and said lightly, but with an undercurrent of determination that could not be ignored, "There, that is all arranged, my dear. I'm sure you will be comfortable, and I'll be in touch with you very shortly." She pressed the electric bell on the table.

"Perkins," she said when her houseman had come up the stairs, "will you get Miss Main a taxi?"

The houseman covered his surprise at sight of the girl by a noncommittal, "Right away."

Beverly looked resentfully at Page and then stared at the jade figurine. "That's funny!" she said sharply. She got up to come to Page, reached out a hand, took the pendant and turned it over and over, examining it closely. "That is exquisite. The groom's gift to the bride, I suppose."

"It's not mine," Vance said. "I only wish I could equal it. We've done things in such a rush we haven't even picked out an engagement ring yet." He looked at Page. "We must do that tomorrow, darling."

"Of course." She smiled at him.

"And not a diamond," he said. "I know enough of your tastes by now —"

"Jade?" she said. "After all, it is the miracle stone."

"You know," Beverly commented, still holding the pendant in a predatory hand so that Page longed to take it away from her, "this reminds me of something."

"I should imagine it to be unique," Vance said. "It's certainly hundreds of years old."

"And yet," Beverly said, "there's a description that exactly fits it somewhere. Now where did I — Oh, I remember. It was in the Lost and Found column. I wouldn't have noticed it, but I lost my wristwatch and I was looking to see whether anyone had found it. And I saw this description. I remember it because of the queer way it was written. The ad said something about $2000 reward and no questions asked. I thought that was rather odd." She gave a sharp look from Page to Vance.

She had done everything short of accusing Page of wearing a piece of jewelry that did not belong to her. For the first time Page realized what Vance had meant about his aunt. Mrs. Wentley's face was cold with anger as she stood, forcing Beverly to get up, to reach for the wrap she had tossed carelessly over a chair. Vance's aunt, Page thought with a twinge of amusement, should have been a top executive. She had handled a sticky situation firmly, without hesitation, and with good manners.

Vance, holding the jacket for a sulky Beverly, observed that it was magnificent mink and looked as though it had never been worn before. As he recalled, the Mains were farmers who barely managed to scratch a living on their Vermont farm and who supplemented their income by pro-

viding board and lodging for hunters and occasional summer people.

Aunt Jane had once accompanied her husband during
the hunting season, and the Mains had nursed her through
an illness. Later, she had agreed to become Beverly Main's
godmother. Vance suspected that she had paid for the
girl's education, but it was highly unlikely that she had provided the mink jacket. He managed to get a look at the
label.

While his hands were still on her shoulders, Beverly
turned with a lithe gesture so that she was practically in
his arms. "I haven't congratulated you on your engagement yet." She kissed his mouth, long and deliberately.

Perkins came up the stairs. "Miss Main's taxi is here,
and there is a telephone call for Mr. Cooper. Will you take
it here, sir?"

Vance's hesitation was only momentary. "Of course,"
he said, after a glance at his aunt for her permission, and
he raised the telephone. At the top of the circular staircase
Beverly paused, drawing on her gloves slowly.

"Cooper speaking . . . Quite right . . . Then I'll be
seeing you — soon." He put down the telephone and smiled
at Beverly's baffled expression. She waved her hand and
ran down the stairs. For a moment he stood looking after
her, wiping his lips with his handkerchief as though trying
to remove all traces of her kiss.

Page, remembering that he had made the flight because
he had an important appointment for the evening, yawned,
apologized, yawned, laughed at herself.

Mrs. Wentley smiled at her. "My dear, you are half asleep
on your feet. Let me show you to your room. And you're

to sleep as long as you like in the morning, of course. When you want your tray, ring for it."

Page forced herself to yawn again, and Vance gave her an approving look. "Aunt Jane is right, as usual. You get a good night's rest." He tipped back her head, brushed her lips lightly with his own. "Sorry I have to go out on your first night."

"If she weren't so tired I would think this was a wretched way to treat her. You drop her in a strange house like a stray kitten and leave her to look after herself." There was only affectionate amusement in Mrs. Wentley's voice, and Vance hugged her gratefully.

"I'm leaving her for you to look after, Aunt Jane." He smiled. "She couldn't be in better hands." He ran down the circular staircase, and a moment later the door closed behind him.

With a smile Mrs. Wentley led the way back to a small bedroom. "This is just a little house," she said, "as I hope Vance warned you, but I got tired of living in that barracks up in Westchester, though I do miss my garden. But there are only three bedrooms here: mine, Vance's, and — yours. I have my small sitting room on this floor and downstairs a drawing room, dining room, kitchen with pantries, and two small rooms for my couple. It's a simple establishment, but I do hope we can make you comfortable."

"It's charming," Page cried in delight, looking around the room with its colonial furnishings, its four-poster bed, rag rugs, the polished lowboy and piecrust table with a bowl of autumn flowers, and a compact bathroom. "Mrs. Wentley, I know Vance said it would be all right, but I think it's a dreadful imposition for him to expect you to take me in, a complete stranger. And I am awfully sorry about upsetting Miss Main's plans. I feel that I have more or less pushed her out."

"It's unfortunate that she failed to get my telegram," Mrs. Wentley said, "but she'll be quite comfortable at the Beekman Towers. Anyhow —" she hesitated for a moment. "I thought I was a fairly sound judge of character, but I am afraid I have been mistaken in Beverly. There is no justification for those — apparent claims she seemed to be making on Vance. None at all." She smiled down at the girl beside her. "As I might have known he would, Vance has chosen well. You have honest eyes, my dear, and character that will wear well. And," her smile deepened, "you are very pretty, which always helps."

"Mrs. Wentley —"

"I think," the tall, stately woman said, "I had better be Aunt Jane to you too. Vance doesn't give his allegiance lightly. If he has given it to you, then you'll have to accept his aunt too."

"Accept her!" Page exclaimed.

"You are welcome here, my dear. Truly welcome."

Page was aware of a pang of guilt. This warm welcome was not for her, it was for the girl who was supposedly going to marry Vance. She could feel herself flushing. She understood now Vance's dislike of deceiving his aunt. Then she remembered Beverly who had waited to listen to Vance's telephone call, Beverly who would be sleeping in this room tonight if it were not for her. That's why I am here, she thought, and her sense of guilt faded.

She stood before the long mirror of her dressing table and removed the jade pendant. For a long time she held it, turning it over and over as Beverly Main had done, remembering what the girl had implied about its being lost or stolen.

One thing was sure. As soon as Leslie returned to San Francisco she would ask her about the jade figurine. Lovely as it was, she began to wish she had never seen the thing.

SIX

THE LOBBY of the huge midtown office building was brilliantly lighted but strangely silent. Except for a few night workers, for cleaning women moving from office to office, the manifold activities of the day were ended. The newsstand was closed. Only one elevator in the half-dozen banks of elevators was running.

Vance Cooper signed his name in the register and then the time of his arrival: ten-ten. The incurious operator took him to the twenty-eighth floor, doors opened and closed silently, and he went along a quiet corridor toward a door behind which light was showing.

He went through a small reception room and down the hall of the big office suite to a room in which he heard voices. Three men were sitting at a small conference table, talking casually while they watched a fourth man who was testing the electrical equipment. The latter climbed off a desk and gave a reassuring nod.

"All clear. So far the place still hasn't been bugged."

"Though how you expect it can be when there is always someone on guard, I can't imagine," one of the men scoffed.

"It appears to be one of our men who is getting his hands on the hush-hush stuff," the first man reminded him dryly.

A telephone rang and one of them answered it. "Oh . . . Get a good look at him? . . . Where . . . Well, I'll be damned . . . Yes, and don't lose sight of him." He set down the telephone and grinned at Vance. "It might interest you to know that you were trailed here. Picked up at your aunt's house. Guy in a light overcoat, suit with a green pin-stripe, and a face like a rat. Ever come across him before?"

"I didn't notice him tonight," Vance admitted, "but I can tell you one thing. He didn't pick me up at my aunt's house. He has been following me all the way from San Francisco."

"Are you sure of that?"

Vance recounted all he knew of Page's story about the ferret-faced man outside Gump's, who had later appeared in the restaurant in San Francisco where they were lunching, and still later tonight at the Plaza in New York where they were dining.

"But why follow you?" one of the men asked. "You don't go around carrying valuable information in your pockets. What's the point?"

"I can't figure that out either," Vance admitted. "I've known for a long time, at least I've been fairly sure, that I was followed here in New York. Frankly I assumed it was our own security branch just making sure I was not talking to the wrong people."

"It wasn't," one of the men said. "Aside from Markham himself, you are the one man completely above suspicion."

"Then," Vance went on, "just before Markham asked me to go out to San Francisco to confer with him, this odd situation about Beverly Main, my aunt's goddaughter, came up. Something about the whole setup bothered me. That's why I asked you to check her out. Did you find anything?"

"Well, you might say so. Four years ago, Beverly Main married a guy from Australia and went down there to live. She has never come back."

"So this girl isn't Beverly Main."

"She isn't. Not by a long shot. From pictures of the real Beverly we gather that their coloring is much alike, and their general build as well. Actually there is not a strong resemblance when you compare their photographs; but you say Mrs. Wentley had not seen the girl since she was five until recently, that she had merely corresponded with her."

Vance nodded. "Have you any idea who she really is? Why is she edging into my aunt's house, or trying to?"

"Her name — at least, the name under which she is living — is Kate Willing. Someone in Williamstown, Massachusetts, where Beverly Main has been supposed to be working, forwards her mail to an apartment here in the Village. I might add that it is a high-priced apartment. She has had it for three months. But there are some things we haven't dug up yet. We don't know where she is getting the money she is spending so lavishly. Above all, we don't know where she has got the background material to fool your aunt. Someone knows a lot about Mrs. Thomas Wentley and Mr. Vance Cooper and has passed that information on to her. That's for sure. Any idea who is priming this girl?"

Vance hesitated. At length he said reluctantly, "My aunt has a daughter Marta. She would be about twenty-three now. She ran away from home five years ago, and if my aunt has heard from her she has never said so."

"You mean she didn't have a search made for her daughter when she disappeared?" The speaker was incredulous.

"I am positive that she did, but she has never mentioned Marta to me since she left home. My aunt is a good woman but not a forgiving one."

"We'll see what we can dig up on the girl but — five

years! What made you think there might be some association between her and this Beverly Main?"

"Tonight Beverly, or whoever she is, made a slip. She said she had expected to have Marta's room. As Aunt Jane never speaks of Marta she got that somewhere else."

After a rather awkward pause one of the men asked, "Do you think your cousin is capable of planting a phony in her mother's house? What could she gain by it?"

"If you mean do I think Marta is capable of involving herself in treachery to her country, the answer is no. If it's a question of trying to make a fool of her mother by proving to her that she can make a mistake, the answer is a tentative yes. But Marta couldn't have bought that mink jacket Beverly is wearing. I made a note of the label, thinking we could trace the buyer."

One man wrote down the name. "We'll look into it and try to trace the buyer."

"Of course, this girl may simply be trying to dig into your aunt's good graces to find out what pickings there are," another suggested. "Would that be possible?"

"As a sideline, perhaps," the third man said. "We've been keeping a sharp eye on this girl ever since Cooper asked us to check on her. It's possible she could be tied up with Operation Homebase. Did you know she returned tonight from San Francisco? Took the flight after yours."

"No!" Vance was startled. "I wonder if that is where she acquired the mink jacket. You don't get that kind with trading stamps. I wonder what someone wanted in exchange for it? At least, we are forearmed now. She can do no further harm; if she has done any."

"If?"

"That's why Markham wanted to talk to me. He appears to have a crackerjack of an agent on the job. He has found out that some of the big stuff has been microfilmed and sent out of the country. He believes a different courier is used each time and sent to a different country. I had an odd feeling that Markham knew more than he was telling me, that his agent had warned him that no one," he grinned wryly, "and I guess that includes me, must know all the facts right now."

"Why don't we put a tail on Ferret-Face and find out to whom he is reporting?"

"That was done automatically as soon as we had a report that he had followed Cooper here. I wonder how many more of them there are?"

Vance recalled Page's saying, half laughing, half dismayed, "I seem to be haunted by fat women in brown coats," and told them of her experiences with the woman in brown.

"You are sure of this Page Wilburn's reliability, are you?"

"Markham is sure. He is the one who chose her."

"Does she strike you as being completely honest?"

"Yes," Vance said sharply. "You have only to look at her to know that."

"And yet," one of the men said slowly, "if her story is to be believed, she was picked up by the ferret-faced man and the woman in brown before there was any public association with you and the Markham company. How do you account for that?"

Seeing Vance's expression the man added hastily, "I realize the old man hasn't made any mistakes about people so far, but there is always a first time."

"The only way I've been able to figure it," Vance said, "is that by some chance Page stumbled on a password. Both of those people were outside Gump's. There is no indication that they are working together, even that they are working for the same country. What we associate with Gump's is jade. And Page tells me that she said, rather casually, to a friend of hers that she could have all the diamonds in the world, but Page would take jade. She referred to it as the miracle stone. In fact, I heard her say that tonight."

He went on to describe her friend's gift of new clothes and the enclosure in the box of the jade figurine, a beautiful and ancient piece of carving, probably priceless, yet hung on a heavy steel chain. For some reason it had not occurred to her to wonder why a clothing shop would be delivering a piece of valuable jewelry. The queer thing was that the seals on the box in which it had been packed were broken when Page received it. Later, someone attempted to snatch the jade figurine in Chinatown, would have dragged Page into a dark alley if a young couple had not come to the rescue.

"Things like that happen every day," a man said impatiently. "I'm darned if I see the connection."

"It's true that they happen every day," Vance admitted, "but the point is that Page was just starting to pass the alley when the attempt was made."

"Meaning?"

"Meaning that the thief had not had the time to see the pendant for which he reached. In other words, he must have been waiting for her to pass. And there is another thing. That jade pendant simply must have a meaning in this business somewhere. Tonight Beverly Main, or Kate Willing, or whoever she is, couldn't take her eyes off it;

she kept fingering it; she asked whether I had given it to Page. Finally she said she had seen a description of a piece of jade exactly like it in a Lost and Found column, offering two thousand dollars' reward for its return and no questions asked. She did everything but say outright that she believed Page had stolen it."

"There's one thing we can settle right now. Who is this friend from whom your Miss Wilburn claims she got it?"

Shrewd eyes watched the color rise in Vance's face, saw his jaw ripple as he controlled his anger at the faint stress on the word *claims*. That's bad, the observant man thought. You can't maintain detachment when you are in love and that is what has happened to Cooper. It must have been one of those first-sight things, though I never believed in them before. Well, we'll simply have to keep a close watch over him and not let the girl out of our sight. His opinion of her isn't to be relied on now.

"Her friend's name is Mrs. Gordon Trevor," Vance said.

One of the men got busy at the telephone. "San Francisco. She ought to be home. What's the time difference — three hours? four hours? I never can remember."

In a remarkably few minutes he was saying, "Mrs. Gordon Trevor, please . . . You are a friend of Miss Page Wilburn? . . . No, she hasn't been hurt. She is quite all right . . . Just a question. Did you recently send her a box containing an outfit of clothes? . . . Will you list the items, please? . . . We have reason to believe the box may have been tampered with . . . Yes . . . yes . . . yes, I have that . . . And that was all? You did not send Miss Wilburn, with the clothing, a jade pendant, a carved figurine probably very ancient and hung on a rather heavy steel

chain? . . . Well, thank you very much . . . Can I what?
. . . Get a message to Miss Wilburn? Just a minute,
please. Cooper, you had better take this. Mrs. Trevor seems
to be greatly upset. I believe she thinks we have snatched
Miss Wilburn away for nefarious purposes."

"Mrs. Trevor? This is Vance Cooper speaking."

"You are the New York man for whom Mr. Markham
wanted Page to do some special work?" The woman's voice
was crisp and angry.

"That's right."

"Is Page in New York with you?"

"She is in New York with my aunt," he said reassur-
ingly, in order to prevent any misunderstanding.

"Look here, Mr. Cooper, something seems to be very
wrong. First, Page goes streaking off to New York practically without warning, just a telephone message. Then, only
a few minutes ago, there was a call from her landlady, who
probably listens in to the telephone calls and knows that I
am Page's closest friend. She was all upset. She said someone broke into the house today and ransacked Page's room,
simply tore it to bits, even slashed the mattress. Nothing else
in the house was touched. She wants to know who is going
to pay for this."

"Did she report it to the police?"

"I don't know. I advised her to do so at once, but she
didn't seem to like the idea. I suppose she is afraid they will
uncover some small violation of the law."

"Please ask her to report immediately. Assure her that
I will be financially responsible for the damage to Miss
Wilburn's room, but do not mention the Markham organi-
zation, will you? We'll make a check of our own."

"All right." Mrs. Trevor was frankly dubious. "Look

here, Mr. Cooper, I've known and loved Page Wilburn all her life. A sister couldn't be dearer to me. She has taken enough punishment. I don't like the sound of this at all. It seems to me that she is being involved in something rather ugly."

"What Page is doing," Vance told her, "is of her own free will. I assure you of that. She is in no danger, Mrs. Trevor. Please believe me."

"Well, heaven help you if she is hurt in some way, Mr. Cooper, because I'll never rest until you are punished for it."

He laughed softly. "I'm glad to know that Page has such a loyal friend. But, Mrs. Trevor, for very serious reasons, I must ask you to say nothing about the jade figurine until you receive permission."

"Permission from whom?" she asked, her voice making clear her suspicion.

"Shall we say — the government?"

There was a small silence. "All right, Mr. Cooper." She sounded rather subdued.

When Vance had related his conversation with Mrs. Trevor and the ransacking of Page's room to the interested men, the quiet man who was in charge of the meeting said, "Well, we know a little more and I think we can guess a lot more. Mrs. Trevor did not give the jade figurine to Miss Wilburn. Someone else put it in her box of clothing, breaking the seals to do so. Later the same person tried to retrieve it, or there are two parties working and the other one tried to get it. Now we seem to have three attempts to get hold of it: one in Chinatown, the woman who tried to get into Miss Wilburn's room in the night, and whoever ransacked her room today in broad daylight."

"And there is also," Vance pointed out, "Beverly Main, the fake Beverly Main, and her passionate interest in that piece of jade, her account of reading a description of it in a Lost and Found column. It's conceivable, isn't it, that if she was in San Francisco, Beverly is actually the courier scheduled to take the microfilm abroad, that there was a mix-up outside Gump's, and Miss Wilburn uttered the password. Which means that that pendant must, in some way, be involved in this business. Perhaps as a matter of identification."

"That, in the words of President Roosevelt, is a bit iffy. And I don't like coincidences."

"Neither do I. But, nonetheless, coincidences happen every day. And always remember, the other side isn't invincible. They can make mistakes. They do make them."

"So what do we do, now?"

"What you do, Cooper, is to get that jade pendant away from Miss Wilburn. Obviously it doesn't belong to her. It is quite possibly a danger to her. It may, quite possibly, be a danger to us."

SEVEN

WHEN PAGE awakened next morning, she looked around her in surprise. Then she remembered. She was in Mrs. Wentley's little house on Murray Hill in New York. There were days of adventure stretching ahead, exciting things to do, clothes to buy, new experiences to have, Vance to escort her.

Ever since Jerry had jilted her she had been alone. She had grown accustomed, but never reconciled, to being the solitary woman wherever she went. Now everything was different. But she must not, she warned herself, forget that this was temporary, she must not become accustomed to an arm to lean on. She had learned by hard experience that the arm could be taken away, without warning, and she would be alone again.

Vance. How long had she known him? Two days? Three days? She remembered her first impression of him as a young man who was able to cope with his world and enjoyed coping. A confident young man without being vain or self-important. Now she found herself comparing him, inevitably, with Jerry. There was no question that Jerry was the better looking, he had an endearing charm. But in some ways he always seemed collegiate, as though he did not really want to grow up. In time of need you'd pick Vance.

And Jerry's attitude on the plane had infuriated her, the kind of insolent challenge with which he had regarded

Vance, as though all he had to do was hold out his hand and Page would come running back to him. "Going your way, Page darling," he had said mockingly. But he had not been mocking when he had telephoned her the day before. There had been something desperate in his voice as though, in spite of everything, he loved her.

Page was sorry for him, she discovered, genuinely sorry, but she was free forever of his spell. Jerry had no power either to make her love him or to hurt her any more.

She looked out of the window at the blue October day, stretched like a lazy cat, and rang the bell for her breakfast tray.

While she sat propped on pillows, sipping coffee and eating flaky croissants, there was a tap on the door and Mrs. Wentley came in.

"Good morning, my dear, I hope you slept well."

"Like a top. Though I've never really understood why a top should sleep."

Mrs. Wentley smiled at her. "Last night you seemed to be exhausted, but this morning you are radiant." She looked at the breakfast tray, with its coffee and hot rolls. "I hope you don't think that's all the breakfast you are expected to have as a rule, but it's nearly eleven and Vance wants you to lunch with him at one. The Pierre. So I thought you'd better not spoil your lunch."

"Nearly eleven!"

"You forget the time difference. It would still be early morning in San Francisco."

"Please sit down," Page said, and the tall woman with the regal bearing sat beside the bed.

"I think," Mrs. Wentley said, "that after your lunch with Vance you had better plan to meet me for a couple of hours of shopping. He explained why you have no wardrobe and I thought I could introduce you to some of the good shops. Vance said something about dinner and a theater tonight, so you'll need things. You'd probably dance later."

"I am being a great nuisance to you," Page said.

"My dear, since my husband's death Vance has been the very core of my life. Like a child of my own. If you could have any idea how happy it makes me to know that you are going to make him happy, that you are making him happy —"

Color rose in a hot flood in Page's face. When Mrs. Wentley knew what a sham she was she would be utterly disgusted, and Page found herself wanting the older woman's good opinion, not just because she was Vance's fiancée but because she was herself, Page Wilburn.

"All I could ever ask," Mrs. Wentley said quietly, "is that you and Vance have the kind of marriage I had. It wasn't merely that we loved each other very much, or that we had so many interests in common, or that we never seemed to run out of things to say to each other. Each of us seemed to — complete the other."

She sat looking out of the window, seeing some vision of her own. Then she said, "I always feel so sorry for the married couples who sit in a restaurant and hardly exchange a word. They haven't anything to say to each other, anything to talk about, no interests to share. I remember the story of the two Supreme Court Justices who were walking down the street in Washington and saw Justice Holmes and his wife in the middle of the street, holding up traffic while they talked. And one Justice said to the other, 'What do you suppose they find to talk about after forty years?' That's my idea of a happy marriage."

"Mine too," Page said.

"You still haven't called me Aunt Jane." Mrs. Wentley smiled at her.

Again Page flushed. "I — wanted to be sure I was really accepted first — Aunt Jane."

"Not like my goddaughter, Beverly, who insists on being accepted," Mrs. Wentley went on dryly. "I must say for Vance that he chose more wisely for himself than I would have chosen for him. I wonder if I made the same mistake with Marta?"

She seemed to be thinking aloud rather than speaking to Page so the latter waited a long time before she dared to comment.

"That's your daughter, isn't it?" she said then, gently.

"Vance told you?"

"Only that — that she doesn't live here now."

Mrs. Wentley sat looking out of the window, her hands clasping each other so that the knuckles were white with pressure.

"Marta," she said slowly at last. "This was her room, furnished for her the way I hoped she would like it. All she said, when she saw it, was that, as usual, I hadn't even respected her wishes enough to consult her taste. She hated old-fashioned stuff. I bought her clothes, lovely clothes. There are two closets filled with them, which she left behind. She said she was old enough to pick out her own clothes."

She turned puzzled eyes on Page. "I failed with Marta. Failed utterly. I don't understand it. Perhaps I was so wrapped up in my husband that I never really knew my daughter. I wanted her to be happy, Page. But I — blundered. When I planned her debut she laughed at me. She said she wasn't going to be trapped by — by an empty life like mine. And then she — went away. She was only eighteen."

After a long pause she said heavily, "And yet I am still sure that I was right, that her values were all wrong, that the life she has chosen for herself will never make her happy."

"Perhaps," Page suggested, timid of expressing an opinion in the face of this heartbreak, "there is no place in love for being right."

"Perhaps that is true," Mrs. Wentley said thoughtfully. "You are a very understanding person, Page."

"And you have never heard from her?"

"She has never got in touch with me, but I know where she is. I had a private detective look for her. She took an apartment in the Village. It's just a slum really, a horrible place, noisy and — and smelly. She has a tiny income of her own, left her by my brother, and she is managing on that somehow. She has refused to accept any financial help from me. Oh, Page, it's such a shoddy life she is leading by choice, when life could be so lovely for her. If only she would come back, if I could know that she is safe, if I could have a share, even the slightest share, in her confidence, in her affection —"

"Mrs. Wentley — Aunt Jane — would you — do you think it would help if I talked to Marta? We're the same age. Perhaps —"

"I don't know. Perhaps it would not help if she knew you came from me. But I would bless you forever if you could bring her back. On her own terms. Any way she wants it. I'll give you her address and try not to — hope too much."

Mrs. Wentley lifted Page's tray from her lap onto a table. "I'll leave you to bathe and dress in peace. Oh, Vance left a note for you this morning." She put it on the dressing table, smiled, and went out.

Page jumped out of bed and opened the note. *Good morning,* it read. *I hope you've had a fine rest because tonight we must celebrate properly or Aunt Jane will wonder what is wrong. Meet me at the Pierre at one for lunch and then we'll get an engagement ring. Your Vance.*

Page frowned over the signature and decided that he had meant to write *Yours.* Though the message was simple enough, for some reason she did not toss it into the wastebasket. She folded it carefully and slipped it into her handbag.

ii

"Well," Page said on a long breath when Vance had finished reporting to her on the previous night's discoveries, "I'd better call Leslie right away and assure her that I am all right."

Vance laughed. "I think, at the very least, she believes you have been kidnaped by some sinister gang. If she isn't sure, she'll probably come gunning for me! She sounded very protective, on the warpath."

"She's a darling and you would like her immensely. But now, at least, we know she had nothing to do with the jade figurine." Page took it in her hand, her fingers caressing the lovely texture. "But who and how and, first and last, why me?"

"First, I'd like to take that pendant to have our laboratory man examine it. Do you mind? No, no! Not now. Not publicly like that. Later."

"After lunch then."

"After lunch our first step will be the bank."

"Bank?"

"Yes, of course." Vance tried to keep his mind on things that must be done, but he found himself losing track of them when he looked into those dark blue eyes, when he watched her brilliant smile. "You've got to get some clothes, and Markham has arranged an account for you here in New York. Your checks will be accepted any place you go with Aunt Jane, and she assures me that she will be delighted to accompany you on a shopping tour and introduce you to the good stores, all that."

"She is very kind, isn't she, to bother so about me when she is so unhappy."

"Unhappy?" Vance echoed in surprise. "I have always regarded her as the most completely self-sufficient woman I know."

"No woman could be completely self-sufficient without — without betraying her own womanhood. She needs people to love or she isn't complete. And your aunt is desperately unhappy, Vance, about Marta."

"She talked to you about Marta? Actually talked about her?" Vance did not conceal his amazement.

Page nodded again. "Marta ran away from home because she felt that she was being managed too much, that her ideas and her thoughts and everything were being controlled by her mother. Now she refuses to accept any help, as though to punish her mother for being over-protective."

"You mean Aunt Jane knows where Marta is and that she has tried to help her?"

"Yes, Marta has an apartment in the Village. Aunt Jane hired a private detective to find her."

"Well!" Vance expelled a long breath. "You have learned more this morning than I've learned in the past five years. How in the world did you do it?"

The waiter brought a chafing dish containing curried chicken and Page said, in heartfelt gratitude, "I'm so glad Aunt Jane wouldn't let me eat much breakfast."

Vance laughed outright. "You're greedy," he accused her.

"Anyone would be greedy with food like this. And I thought San Francisco was the perfect place for restaurants."

"You haven't seen anything yet," he boasted. "We'll try a different nationality every night. We're going to make food an adventure."

Page, looking hastily down at her plate, thought in wonder, "A meal at a hamburger stand would be adventure with him. Being with Jerry was never like this. Never in the world."

Aware of her uncertain and treacherous color, which came and went, she said quickly, "Vance, I can't wait to get rid of this pendant, lovely as it is. There is something wrong about it. If my room in San Francisco was ransacked it must have been in search of the pendant. And mine, you said, was the only room that was entered."

"According to what your landlady told Mrs. Trevor."

"Then it must have been the fat woman in brown. The one who watched that night and tried — I am sure she tried — to get into my room. I felt the doorknob turn under my hand, felt a board in the floor move when she went down." Page shivered, and her eyes seemed bigger than ever as she recalled that moment of fear.

"I don't know who it was, but we're going to do our

best to find out. What would you like for dessert? . . .
Nothing? . . . Sure? . . . Then we'd better get busy and
do our errands."

In the taxi on the way to the bank Vance said quietly,
"Page, who are the friends who suggested that you work
for Markham Electronics?"

The brilliant smile faded. She came back to earth with
a jolt that jarred her right back to reality. Her relationship with Vance was just a smoke screen and there was
nothing behind it. Not even trust, she thought bitterly, angry
with herself for having begun to see a new, shining future.

"One of them," she said, her voice so cold that he looked
at her in surprise, "is Ted Harvest, Theodore Harvest,
who works in the San Francisco branch. The other is Norman Graham, who has recently been transferred to the New
York office."

"What can you tell me about them?" Vance asked, and
there was no trace of the laughter-warmed friendship of a
few minutes ago. This was a stranger with a job to do.

"I really can't tell you much." She tried to speak with
detachment. "I knew them only because of Alice and
Helen, the two dearest friends I have in the world, aside
from Leslie, of course. Somehow, until I went to Peru, we
were always together. Alice married Ted Harvest. Something seems to have gone wrong with the marriage because
the last I heard of her she had come to New York alone.
Helen was engaged to marry Norman Graham and then the
engagement was broken. He is in the New York office now.
I want to make one thing crystal clear, Vance. I don't
know anything against either man. I like them both and I
don't believe, for a single minute, that they are betraying

their country or stealing the secrets of Markham Electronics."

Vance looked at her, puzzled by her manner. Then, as the taxi drew up at the bank, he got out to give her a hand. An account had already been established for her. When Page had filled out some forms, been provided with a checkbook, and cashed her first check, Vance tucked her hand under his arm and steered her up Fifth Avenue. He almost rushed her past a fascinating display in a window in spite of her protests.

"Not now," he told her. "I'll have to get back to the office, but first we must choose that engagement ring."

"Vance, Mr. Markham should not have deposited so much money in that account for me."

"You needn't spend it all, but you'll have to get some evening clothes, afternoon clothes, a suit or two, some sports clothes, and certainly a warm coat. It's not such a whale of a lot of money, as you'll soon find out. Anyhow," he smiled at her, "just remember that you can return what you don't need."

As he turned in at the famous doorway Page's eyes widened. Cartier's.

He dragged her, laughing, away from a display of brooches.

"What may I show you?" a clerk asked, smiling.

"An engagement ring," Vance said.

The clerk looked at Page. "I congratulate you," he said. "The diamonds are over here, sir."

"Not diamonds." Vance was firm. "My fiancée prefers jade."

The clerk nodded. "That's a magnificent piece she is

wearing. The kind of thing you don't often see out of a museum. Wonderful carving. May I —?"

As Page nodded permission he examined it closely, and then whipped out a glass. "What a pity that there should be a flaw in it. At first I thought it might be part of the carving but —"

"Flaw!" Vance exclaimed, reached for the pendant which Page removed and handed him with an obscure feeling of relief. Lovely as it was she had grown afraid of it.

Vance thrust it into his pocket and began to look at the jade rings. The one he finally selected, though the price appalled Page, was a soft pink, like a cloud just barely touched by the setting sun.

"May I keep this pendant for a while?" he asked as he put Page in a cab.

"Keep it forever!" she said feelingly.

"Get a dress to match the ring." He smiled deep into her eyes and then, abruptly, he was gone.

iii

Behind closed doors the two men examined the jade figurine. The man with the glass looked up to say, "There's a crack, all right." Carefully he inserted the thin blade of a knife. Nothing happened. He moved the point of the knife up and down the crack, came back to the spot in the center.

"There is something here, something rough that catches the knife-blade. My guess is that it is a tiny spring. Ah!" he exclaimed in satisfaction.

The figurine opened, not through the middle as he had expected but like a Fabergé Easter Egg. The interior had been hollowed out and contained a tiny receptacle no larger than a kidney bean.

Again the glass came into play.

"What is it?" Vance demanded hoarsely.

"Looks like a microfilm. Give us a little while in the lab and I'll have a report for you."

While he was gone, Vance went restlessly back to his office. In a few minutes he was joined by one of the men with whom he had conferred the night before. He explained that he was waiting for a report on the microfilm that had been concealed in the jade figurine.

The other man was jubilant. "It looks as though we have retrieved the stuff before it could get into enemy hands. We'll make sure that nothing else is filmed. Apparently this Page Wilburn was mistaken for the real courier. That's the only way I can account for it. By the way, have you found out who her friends in the company are?"

"A Theodore Harvest in the San Francisco office, whose marriage seems to be on the rocks, and a Norman Graham who has recently been transferred here from San Francisco and whose engagement has been broken."

"We'll go over them with a fine-tooth comb," the man promised. He looked up as the scientist returned.

"We've got it!" the latter said triumphantly.

"Operation Homebase?"

"As ever was. It would never have occurred to me to try to take apart a piece of woman's jewelry."

"Then you think the courier must have been intended to be a woman?"

"It would have to be. A man carrying a thing like this would be bound to arouse attention. He would have to explain. Well, thank God, we've saved it."

"That's true, but up to now no one but the three of us knows that we have the microfilm in our hands."

Vance looked at the speaker without comprehension.

"The only way we can smoke out our traitor is to make him go after that jade figurine again."

"Oh, no!" Vance exploded wrathfully.

"Look here, Cooper, there's a whole lot more at stake than the girl, though we'll do everything that is humanly possible to protect her. She will be under observation every minute. But I want you to give her back that pendant."

"Staked out like a lamb for the slaughter. No! Not under any conditions."

"I don't like it any better than you do," the other man admitted, "but this is war, and in time of war no civilian can be entirely safe. You know that as well as I do. I don't insist that the girl wear the figurine all the time. That isn't necessary. What is essential is that everyone be made to believe it is still in her possession — and still intact."

"At least," Vance said after a long time, "she must be given the right to make the choice. She must understand that what she is being asked to do may be dangerous. She has got to know what she is up against and be willing to do it."

"Fair enough." The other man reached for the telephone. "I want that twenty-four-hour guard kept on Page Wilburn until further notice. We'll need at least two people for this job at all times. There must be no slip-up."

He set down the telephone, pushed the now harmless pendant across the table to Vance who pocketed it.

"You know," the man said, trying to speak lightly, to lift Vance's furious mood, "this is going to be quite a parade: Page Wilburn, our two shadows, the ferret-faced man who is still on your track. Our men reported that Ferret-Face seemed to be entranced by your actions in Cartier's. He didn't stay so long in the bank, just long enough to find out what was going on. Banks don't encourage loiterers."

"I didn't even notice him," Vance admitted, chagrined at having missed this chance to examine the fellow carefully.

His colleague gave him an ironic look. "Apparently your attention was otherwise occupied. Our information is that the Wilburn girl is a raving beauty. Look here, Cooper, there's no sense in beating around the bush. Let's get through the next four weeks and keep our minds on the job, shall we? After that, if you want to develop some personal interests, that will be fine with us. But first things first. All right?"

"All right, but God help you if anything happens to Page!"

EIGHT

THE SHOP was inconspicuous enough from the outside, just a simple nameplate on the door, though the name was world-famous. The window itself held no displays; it was covered with heavy gray drapes.

"I'd never have guessed this was a famous dress shop," Page admitted, as she followed Mrs. Wentley into the long, narrow room.

The interior did not seem much like a dress shop either. There was wall-to-wall carpeting that matched the drapes; there were a few chairs covered in pale green velvet; there were small tables. The lighting was in soft peach, which, the astute dressmaker had learned long ago, was most becoming to women.

The saleswoman who came forward was middle-aged, smartly dressed in black, with a narrow, clever face.

"This is a pleasure, Mrs. Wentley. We haven't seen you since last spring. We began to think you were abroad."

"Later, perhaps, but I expect to be here until at least the first of the year."

"What may I show you? Do sit down."

When they were seated, Mrs. Wentley said, "Miss Wilburn is going to marry my nephew, and she has flown here from San Francisco to buy her trousseau."

The woman's face remained impassive, but her eyes shone. A whole trousseau!

"It will be a joy to dress Miss Wilburn. The only trouble is that there is no challenge in making her look well. Where do we start?"

"Miss Wilburn is just out of mourning," Mrs. Wentley went on, taking charge because Page was hesitant, "so she has to start practically from scratch. But first she needs something for tonight, for a theater and dancing."

"Any choice of colors?"

Page removed her glove and displayed her engagement ring. "A soft rose-pink that will match this jade ring," she said, "if it is possible to find something suitable." She turned glowing eyes on Mrs. Wentley. "That's what Vance said he wanted."

"Then," Mrs. Wentley assured her with a smile, "that is what you should have, though I expect he'd be satisfied no matter what you wore."

The saleswoman went out, there were murmured words, and then she returned. One by one, the models came in, walked slowly, turned, then came near so Page could examine the fabrics, moved away so she could study the lines from a distance.

"Oh, this one," she decided at last, "that is, if it fits me. There won't be time for alterations, I'm afraid."

In the fitting room she looked at herself in the three-way mirror, at the dress like a pink cloud that seemed to add color to her cheeks, depth to her eyes, make her hair seem a richer shade. She studied the long, swirling lines of the skirt that swept the floor, the perfect fit of the bodice, her gleaming arms and shoulders.

When she went out into the salesroom, Mrs. Wentley looked at her and exclaimed, "Good heavens, I didn't realize how beautiful you are! If there is anything left of

Vance's heart for you to win, he is going to lose it tonight."
She laughed. "And it doesn't need a thing. It fits like a
glove."

Back in her gray outfit, with its green accessories, Page
watched the models come and go. Following Mrs. Wentley's advice, she selected another evening dress, this one of
white with long, straight lines, two afternoon dresses, a
wool skirt and matching shirt and sweater in bittersweet.

Suits, she was told, should be made for her by a tailor.
Now they would have to dash to get shoes to match the
evening dress. Coats, wraps, gloves, must wait for another
day.

Though it was well past five, the saleswoman was smiling
brightly when they left, putting the suitbox in a taxi. It
was while she was standing back to let Mrs. Wentley precede her into the cab that Page noticed the ferret-faced man,
and some of the radiance that had engulfed her all day
faded. She recalled that there must be a midnight for Cinderella, that this incredibly happy and glamorous day, the
fabulous clothes, the kindness of Aunt Jane, and the —
well, the attentive kindness of Vance, were all part of a world
she must leave within four weeks.

"What's wrong, my dear?" Aunt Jane spoke gently, as
the taxi turned down Park Avenue and into the late-after-
noon traffic that moved sluggishly, bumper to bumper. "I'm
afraid we have attempted to do too much at one time. We
should have been satisfied with the evening dress and slippers for tonight."

"Nothing is wrong," Page assured her. She summoned
up a bright smile. She was still smiling gallantly when Perkins admitted them to the house on Murray Hill and took
the suitbox from her.

"There is a gentleman waiting," he said, indicating the drawing room.

"For me?" Mrs. Wentley asked. "Who is it?"

"No, for Miss Wilburn. He didn't give me a name. He just said he was an old friend."

The man who stood up as they entered the drawing room was Jerome Brooks. Now Page's smile faded entirely. For a long moment they looked at each other and she saw in his face something of the desperation she had heard in his voice over the telephone.

As a result, she was kinder than she had intended to be. "Aunt Jane," she said, "may I present Jerome Brooks, a — an old acquaintance of mine from San Francisco. Mrs. Wentley, Jerry."

"How do you do?" Mrs. Wentley said.

For the first time Page was aware of what an imposing personality the older woman had. Because she had revealed only warmth and a relaxed kindness to Page, the latter had not realized that the tall, stately woman could be so forbidding. Even when she had been annoyed with Beverly Main she had handled the situation with kindness and tact. But Jerry, always self-confident where women were concerned, was aware of her barrier of frigid reserve.

For a moment there was an oddly sardonic expression on the good-looking face as he bowed to the older woman.

Perkins came in from the back of the house with a tall vase filled with fragrant long-stemmed roses. "The gentleman brought these for you, Miss Wilburn."

"They are beautiful. Thank you, Jerry."

Mrs. Wentley looked from one face to the other and then, with a nod, started up the stairs. She paused to say, "You ought to get some rest before dressing for dinner, my dear."

"I will, Aunt Jane." Page looked at Jerry. "I'll be up in just a few minutes."

And then they were alone. Her voice and expression were cold as she asked, "What are you doing here, Jerry?"

"Don't sound like that, so cold, so impersonal. As though we were strangers. I wanted to see you. I told you — remember? — that I was going your way."

She looked at him with detachment. The magic was quite gone. The Byronic profile, the caressing voice, the charming smile seemed to have lost their effect.

She paused for a moment as Perkins came in, hesitated, and then went upstairs. Then she spoke decisively. "It's too late, Jerry. Six months too late. How did you find me?"

"Your landlady heard you talk on the telephone. That is how I knew you were going to New York, what flight you would be on, where you would be staying."

"I told you I was going to marry Vance Cooper."

"You can't marry him, Page! I'm the man you love. We've loved each other for two years. You don't forget a love like that overnight. You can't."

"Apparently you could," she reminded him. "Anyhow, this is all unnecessary, all beside the point."

"Don't be so hard, darling!" The caressing note was in his voice. "And please don't just hover there. Won't you let me sit down just for a few minutes? Just ten minutes. I don't ask much."

"Ten minutes then. But after that I must rest before I dress for dinner." Page sat down, hoping devoutly that Jerry would leave before Vance came home. She pulled off her gloves and Jerry caught his breath when he saw the soft pink jade ring on her engagement finger.

He held her eyes then, the color fading from his face.

"You really intend to marry this man?" he asked incredulously. "What has changed you?"

"I might ask the same thing," she replied. "After all, I am still penniless, you know. And, as you made abundantly clear, you must marry a rich girl."

"Page! Forgive me. Can't you forgive me? None of that matters any more. I don't care whether you have a cent. I don't care about the diplomatic career. I don't care about anything but you."

He broke off as Perkins came down the circular staircase, looked swiftly from one to the other, and then went to the back of the house. Page wondered uneasily whether their voices had carried, whether Mrs. Wentley had heard what they were saying.

"I don't want to be unkind," she said at last, "but there would be no kindness in pretending. Whatever feeling I had for you is — finished, Jerry. It's all over." She stood up, forcing him to get to his feet. "Please go now, and don't come back. There's no place in my life for you. No place here."

Again, for a fleeting moment, amusement warred with what she believed to be his genuine chagrin and disappointment. He took her left hand in his, looked at the exquisite stone in the engagement ring.

"Wonderful jade," he said. "You seem to go in rather heavily for jade these days, don't you?"

At that moment Page noticed the heavy signet ring on his left hand. She had, of course, seen it many times during the months of their courtship and engagement. But now, in conjunction with his renewed interest in her, his reference to jade, she stared at his ring, her eyes widening with speculation. Could it have been Jerry who had attacked her in Chinatown? Could it be the jade pendant, which, like the Pied Piper, seemed to draw a variety of creatures in its wake by some irresistible attraction, that had drawn him back into her orbit? Nonsense. The thing was ridiculous.

She withdrew her hand, pressed a button against the wall and, when Perkins appeared, said, "Mr. Brooks is leaving now."

Jerry looked at her for a dismayed moment as though he could not believe she would actually dismiss him, and then he said, almost as though challenging her, "I'll see you again — soon, Page," and went through the doorway.

When Perkins had closed the outer door behind him Page said, "Please do not admit Mr. Brooks again, Perkins. Not for any reason whatever," and went swiftly upstairs.

To her surprise she found Mrs. Wentley waiting for her in the upstairs sitting room. In one swift glance the older woman observed the girl's flushed face, but she made no comment on her visitor.

"My dear," she said in concern, "the strangest and most upsetting thing has happened. Perkins tells me that when his wife, who doubles as housemaid as well as cook, went up to your room this afternoon, she found that someone had been searching it."

"Searched!" Color ebbed from Page's face.

"The strangest thing is that nothing else in the whole house has been disturbed or tampered with in any way. I don't understand it."

Her manner was impeccable but Page, seeing the worry, the concern in the older woman's face, knew that she was linking in her mind Beverly's story of the lost pendant with the searching of the room. Her faith in Page was badly shaken. It was obvious, too, that she had not liked the young man who had brought the magnificent roses and who had seemed to be staking a claim to Page.

"I suppose I had better call the police at once," Mrs. Wentley said, still watching her.

"Wait until you have talked to Vance about it," Page suggested. "He will know what to do."

NINE

WHEN she had dressed, the soft, rose-pink dress falling over her shoulders in a frothy cloud, Page stood looking at herself in the mirror. She had never been lovelier in her life, and she knew it. For a long time she stood turning the pink jade ring around and around, remembering the moment in Cartier's when Vance had slipped it on her finger and the clerk had moved discreetly away. Of course, four weeks from now she would have to return it, but now—

There was a tap at the door and she called, "Come in."

Vance in evening clothes stood looking at her, his eyes widening. "You're beautiful!" he exclaimed. He added, "Aunt Jane told me about your room being searched. Perkins and I have been going over the locks. There's no sign of their being forced or scratched. I don't know what to make of it. Anything gone?"

She shook her head and went out to the small sitting room. Mrs. Wentley's bedroom door was closed, and they were alone.

"Your aunt wanted to call the police but I thought — that is, I suggested that she wait to know what you wanted to do about it."

"What I can't figure out is how they got in the house unless someone has a key. But at least," he said grimly, "we know what they were looking for."

"They?"

"The organization that has been taking such an interest in you."

She nodded without surprise. "The ferret-faced man followed me again today. I saw him less than two hours ago."

"Just remember, Page, that he isn't the only one. There are also two security men who are keeping an eye on you."

"What's wrong, Vance? They couldn't steal the pendant because it wasn't here. You had it."

He reached into his pocket, drew it out, the ugly steel chain dangling from his fingers. He showed her the almost invisible crack where the spring was hidden, told her what the secret compartment contained.

"So the microfilm is safe!" Page expelled a long breath of relief, but there was no answering relief in Vance's face.

"The microfilm is safe," he agreed, "but, as my superiors pointed out to me today, only three of us know that it is safe. They —" He came to a dead stop.

After a long pause, while she searched his face, Page said steadily, though her color had faded, "Let me guess. The Markham people want someone to make another attempt to get hold of the pendant, don't they? The carrot before the donkey."

"You don't have to do it!" he said quickly. "I made that a condition before even asking you. You have every right to make the choice. These people are playing for keeps, Page. Even if we watch them constantly, there is always a chance — there's a risk — a danger —"

There was no hesitation in her voice or her manner. "I told you I was a coward, and that's true, in a way, Vance. But men going into battle are afraid, too. And men are going into battle every day. This is my war as well as theirs. I'll take back the pendant. Even when I'm not wearing it I'll take care to mention it to everyone I see and say that it is in my possession." She added quickly, "but, of course, I won't attach any importance to it, aside from the beauty of the jade itself."

"Are you sure you are willing to do this?"

"I'm sure."

He took an impulsive step toward her, and she found herself swaying toward him with an impulse she only half understood. Then he said, his voice under control, the warm light gone from his eyes, "Shall I put it on for you?"

He clasped the chain round her neck, the jade figurine hung against the soft cloud-pink of the dress. For a moment his fingertips lingered against her warm throat and then his hands dropped as though he had been burned.

"Aunt Jane," he said briskly, "says you have had no time to get an evening wrap. There's an ermine cape belonging to Marta that she thought might do." He let it fall over her shoulders. "Well," he tried to laugh, "off to the wars."

"Off to battle," she said gaily. Then she began to laugh. "Oh, Vance! Not like that! You look like the Charge of the Light Brigade. 'Into the Valley of Death rode the four hundred.' Let's keep the evening gay, shall we?"

ii

Here and there, people turned in the restaurant for a look at the handsome young couple, the girl as lovely and sweet as a wild rose, the man's adoring eyes intent on her face, watching every expression.

"How rarely one sees real happiness," a man said to his companion. "People can be gay, or deeply interested, or even rather maudlin about each other without — without that special quality those two have found together."

"I know," the woman with him said. "And I hope with all my heart they can keep it forever."

"Forever? That's a long time. To have had it at all, even to have caught a glimpse of it for a fleeting moment, is more than most people ever know."

And yet Page was aware, for all the admiration in Vance's eyes, for all his gay talk, that he was not in a happy mood. Now and then the long-lashed lids lifted suddenly and detected something that was not admiration in his face. A question. Almost a doubt.

He spoke abruptly. "Aunt Jane tells me you had an unexpected caller this afternoon."

She nodded. "Unexpected is right. It was Jerry Brooks. You know, Vance, I can't understand it. People don't change like that. Jerry didn't want to marry me because I had no money. I still have no money. But now, all of a sudden, he claims that it doesn't make any difference, that he doesn't even care about his career. No, I simply can't understand it. In any case, I asked Perkins not to admit him again."

Some of the doubt vanished from Vance's face. "I wondered why he had come. So, I suspect, did Aunt Jane. She said he had rather a proprietary manner toward you and I believe she resented it on my account."

Page made a helpless gesture and the pink jade ring glowed in the light. "Vance, you'll really think I'm crazy but this afternoon I wondered —"

"Well?" He was smiling, like himself again.

"I haven't any money. That part hasn't changed in the slightest. But — I do have the pendant, which is probably worth more than any money I ever had. At least it was while it held the microfilm. And Jerry wears a heavy signet ring on his left hand."

He sat frowning at her, thinking it over. "You mean he may be the one who attacked you in Chinatown? Jerome Brooks? The guy who is headed for a diplomatic career and jettisoned you to get it?" He looked up as the waiter hovered, flourishing the big menus.

"What will you have for dessert?"

"Crêpes suzette," she decided. "I love watching them set alight."

Vance laughed. "If a good digestion is a sign of a good disposition, you must have the best."

"Go ahead and laugh," she said, smiling at him. "For four weeks I intend to eat all the wonderful food I can to make up for all those past months of hamburgers and canned spaghetti." And all the months ahead of the same diet, she thought, but put the idea away from her.

When the waiter had deftly prepared the crêpes suzette, spooned the flaming sauce over them, and gone, Page, in spite of her appetite, put down her fork.

"There are little things I can't account for," she said. "Intangible things."

"Let's take a look at them," he suggested.

When she had listed them they didn't, she admitted to herself, amount to much. Jerry's signet ring, though any number of men wore rings; his knowledge that both Page and Vance were employed by the Markham Electronics Company; his interest in her sudden acquisition of jade; an odd, covert amusement in his face when he spoke either of Vance or of his aunt, as though he knew something to their discredit.

"Something is wrong. I feel it," she concluded.

"Aunt Jane!" Vance said wrathfully.

"Yes, it was almost as though he knew something against her and it amused him."

"That," Vance said, "is preposterous."

"What big words you know!" said a laughing voice, and Page turned in surprise to see the tall bronzed man who had paused beside the table, accompanied by a handsome woman.

As Vance had said, Miles Forrest in New York was very different from the Miles Forrest of San Francisco. He was dressed in beautifully tailored evening clothes and the woman beside him looked as though she were dressed by Dior.

Vance stood up and the two men shook hands. Miles beamed at Page. "Ruth, this is Vance's fiancée. Hasn't he picked himself a world-beater?"

The woman looked at Page and there was a question in her face, almost a kind of hostility. "I'm beginning to be jealous," she said, and she wasn't altogether joking. "Miles has been raving about you. I hope Vance will bring you to dinner some evening. I'll give you a ring as soon as I can get to my calendar." After a few minutes the couple went on.

Page shook her head, baffled. "He is like two different men, isn't he?"

"No, Miles is always the same. It's just this kid stuff about dressing the part. He's solid gold, as I think you will find, and I believe you'll like his wife too. They married just after he left college and it's a good marriage."

Vance looked across the table at Page, a puzzled expression on his face. "They have always seemed to me to be a really united couple but, for some reason, she is jealous of you, Page. I realize any woman could be; there isn't a girl in the room who can touch you. But I had the strangest feeling that she was jealous before she met you. You saw Miles only that one time?"

"When he nearly knocked me over," Page laughed.

Vance glanced at his watch. "Curtain goes up at eight-fifty. We'd better be on our way."

When he had slipped the ermine cape over her bare shoulders he paused for a moment, pointing out the lights of New York before moving toward a taxi.

"A penny for them," he said.

"I was just wondering about our theme song."

"What's that?"

"I wonder who's watching us now."

iii

All her life Page Wilburn would remember that evening. Even at the time she was aware of her happiness, happiness that glowed from within and made her beautiful. She had dreamed dreams before and had seen them fade in disillusionment. Now, when she had accepted a strange and disturbing job, when she had expected little or nothing from it, she seemed to find all her senses more alert, to see more clearly, to feel more deeply than ever in her life.

But, as nothing can be perfect, there was one shadow on that miraculous night. Though Vance was delightful and entertaining, though she was aware that he admired her and enjoyed being with her and was proud of her, there was a curious restraint in his manner. Half a dozen times, a spontaneous word or gesture was checked, as though there were an invisible barrier between them, a barrier Vance could not — or did not want to ? — cross.

The play was intelligent, well acted and highly amusing. Later they danced, after enjoying one of the wittiest entertainers in New York.

During those hours Page forgot everything but the joy of the moment, except for a couple of trivial incidents, both of which occurred as they were leaving the hotel where they had been dancing.

The first was when Page, in the woman's room, was powdering her nose and running a comb through her hair. In the mirror she became aware of the young woman behind her, reflected in the glass, of the eyes that summed her up as though photographing her, that looked at the jade figurine and then away again.

Unconsciously she pulled the ermine cape closer around her shoulders, feeling a cold chill. She had forgotten that, from now on, there would be eyes on her.

The other incident occurred as Vance was taking her out of the hotel.

"Taxi, sir?" the doorman asked.

As Vance turned, a young man behind him bumped into him and apologized. A rather long apology, it seemed to Page.

"No taxi," Vance said. He turned to Page. "I took a chance and had my own car delivered. This is my night, you know, and I don't want it to end yet. I thought you might enjoy riding for a while, looking at the lights of Manhattan, all that."

"I'd love it!" Page exclaimed.

When they had drawn away from the curb and into the

traffic, much lighter at this time of night, he asked, "Warm enough?"

"Just fine," she assured him. "Vance?"

"Yes, my — yes, Page?"

"What was all that about in the lobby? The man who pretended to bump into you?"

"Oh." Vance laughed. "You don't miss much, do you? He identified himself as one of the security agents who is keeping an eye on you."

"I'd almost forgotten about the watching eyes," she said, "though there was a girl in the woman's room who stared at me in the most searching way, almost as though she were trying to memorize my face, feature by feature."

Vance laughed softly. "There was hardly a person in that hotel who wasn't staring at you. In fact, you are quite something, Miss Wilburn!"

"Thank you, Mr. Cooper."

But again that invisible barrier seemed to stop him and he fell silent. They drove through the night, the wind cool on Page's face, lifting her soft hair.

Little by little they began to talk, not about war and peace, about city problems and all the ills that beset mankind, but about the important things. They talked about the games they had played as children, about what they had planned to do "when they grew up," about his college days at Dartmouth when Miles Forrest was the hero of his class, about her experiences in Peru and her beloved father. And they laughed a lot. It occurred to Page that she had laughed more in the past few days with Vance than she had in many months.

And then they were crossing the George Washington Bridge, looking down on the broad sweep of the Hudson

River; turned, and came back so that they could see the un-sleeping lights of the city.

They were silent now as they drove down the Henry Hudson Parkway, turned east, and went down Park Avenue, past towering apartment buildings, around Grand Central Station, down to the Murray Hill house.

Abruptly Vance asked, "Are you still unhappy about Jerry, Page?"

She turned her head sleepily on the back of the seat. "Who?" she asked absently, as though she had come back from a great distance.

"Nothing." After a moment Vance began to whistle softly to himself.

TEN

*A*GAIN Page slept late. It had been nearly four o'clock in the morning when Vance unlocked the door of the Wentley house and took her up to her room. At the door he hesitated, then said abruptly, "Good night, Page," and his own door opened and closed behind him.

There was an odd pang of disappointment. She had expected him to kiss her. After all, they were engaged, weren't they? Then she stumbled into her room, nearly half asleep. Just time to undress and brush her teeth and she tumbled into bed. Almost immediately she slept deeply.

When she awakened late in the morning, very late, she lay looking at the ceiling, reliving the previous evening, moment by moment. There was a Swiss proverb, she recalled: "I have that in my pocket." It meant this was something that no one could take away.

She stretched her arms over her head, let them fall lazily on the bed, lifted her left hand to look at the soft pink jade of the ring she wore. Some of the brightness died out of her face. This was something that could be taken away. When the engagement came to the end of its usefulness she must give the ring back to Vance. She thrust the thought away from her. Plenty of time to think of that later. Plenty of time in which to realize that she would never, in all probability, see Vance again. When this job was finished —

And then she knew what had happened to her. She had fallen in love with Vance Cooper.

All right, she told herself defiantly, someday this is going to hurt. But Leslie said Dad faced all experience, even when it hurt. At least, for this minute — and after all, you live only one minute at a time — I'm happy.

This morning there was no note from Vance. Instead, when her breakfast tray was brought to her room there was a note from Mrs. Wentley.

My dear, Vance tells me you were terribly late getting in. That isn't a criticism. I do hope you had fun. So you are to rest as long as you like today. I have a committee meeting of the League of Women Voters to attend this morning and later a luncheon. I hope you don't mind being left on your own like this. Affectionately, Aunt Jane.

Page reread the note slowly. "This isn't a criticism." How anxious she had been to make that clear. Poor Aunt Jane! Surely there must be some way of making Marta see how deeply she had wounded her mother. Whatever disagreement had occurred between the two women must be long forgotten. All that remained would be a memory of anger, of resentment, of bitterness. Remembering her own bitterness, so recently discarded, Page was ashamed of herself. But could she hope to help Marta, whom she did not know, as Leslie, whom she had long loved and trusted, had helped her? At least she could try. When this month was over it would be good to know that something pleasant was the result, something that would endure.

She dressed in the new bittersweet skirt and shirt, brushed her hair until the soft waves shone with light, put on her warm sweater and low-heeled shoes. She had a whole day ahead of her; well, she corrected herself after a glance at her watch, a whole afternoon. What would she do with it? At first she thought of sauntering along Fifth Avenue, looking in shop windows, perhaps going to a museum. Then she recalled the jade pendant, the watching eyes. Her spirits quailed. The purpose of the pendant was to attract the enemy. Tomorrow, she promised herself. Not today.

But first there was something she must do, something urgent. In Aunt Jane's little sitting room she put in a call for Leslie Trevor in San Francisco.

"Page!" Leslie exclaimed, in delight and relief. "I've nearly perished with anxiety and curiosity. What is this all about? First, you rush off to New York. Next, your room here is ransacked. My dear, even the mattress was slashed! Your landlady was practically apoplectic with rage about it. Then I get a mysterious telephone call from New York, asking about the clothes I sent you and saying something about a jade pendant. What jade pendant, for heaven's sake! Are you harboring stolen goods? And then, on top of everything else, your Vance Cooper comes on the telephone — he does sound so nice, Page! — and asks me not to say anything about anything to anybody, whispering mysterious words about the government. You start talking, girl, before I go out of my mind!"

Long before this diatribe had ended Page was helpless with laughter. Poor Leslie! She must feel that her friend was taking part in a Grade B movie.

"First," she said, "he is just as nice as he sounds, but he isn't my Vance." And then she wondered why that had come first. "But you mustn't let anyone guess that. We're supposed to be engaged."

"Supposed to be !"

"Look, Leslie, there is a lot I can't explain right now."

"Oh, not you too !" Leslie wailed.

"But you have my word that everything is all right. Perfectly all right. I am staying with Vance's aunt, who couldn't be nicer to me, and who is the kind of chaperon even a Victorian matron of the most rigid sort would approve of."

"Well," Leslie said doubtfully, "if you are quite sure —"

"Quite sure."

Leslie expelled a sigh of relief. "One thing I know. You would never lie to me. So that is all right."

"Of course it is. By the way, Leslie, you know how I lost touch with Alice and Helen, with everyone except you."

"And how well I know ! Just because of that horrible Jerry."

"Which reminds me," Page said casually, "that Jerry is here in New York."

"In New York ! What is he doing there ?"

"He said that he was going my way," Page told her.

"Page Wilburn, if you let him worm his way back into your good graces after the way he behaved, I'll never forgive you."

"You needn't worry. But tell me about Alice and Helen."

"Things are a mess with both of them," Leslie admitted unhappily. "I thought Ted Harvest and Alice were terribly in love, but here they've been married only a little over a year and he is slaving away in San Francisco and she has gone off to New York by herself. A vacation, she said. She told me she owed it to herself. No use being stuck in that apartment just because Ted thought his work more important than his wife. I wish you'd look her up, Page. Somehow, you have a way of finding the right thing to say. I ran into Ted the other day and made him have dinner with us. He couldn't be made to utter a word of criticism of Alice, of course, but he did admit he was sort of tired of cooking his own dinners. I could shake her!"

"What's her New York address?"

"Somewhere near Riverside Drive and quite far uptown, I think. Oh, here it is." Leslie read aloud the address and Page wrote it down.

"And what about Helen?"

"Well, what went wrong there I just don't know," Leslie admitted. "She and I lunched together last week. She didn't even mention Norman Graham, and she isn't wearing her engagement ring and is very down in the mouth. Whatever their quarrel was about she doesn't feel a bit happy, I can tell you that."

"I'm sorry," Page said. "I thought that engagement would work out."

"By the way, did you know that Norman has been transferred to the New York office of Markham? Oh, yes, of course you would. Anyhow, at last I asked her bluntly what had gone wrong. She said all her life she had had to do without things and so had her mother because her father was so extravagant there was never enough money left for the house expenses. So when Norman bought himself a Cadillac and began having his clothes tailormade, even his shirts, she gave him back his ring. She had had enough of careless spending to last her a lifetime and she wasn't going to pinch and scrape, as her mother had done, so her husband could spend everything on himself and deprive them of any security."

"That's odd," Page said in surprise. "It doesn't sound in

the least like Norman Graham to try to make a splurge."

After she had put the telephone down she sat looking at it thoughtfully, unaware of the view from the window of the buildings across the street, of traffic. How had Norman Graham managed to acquire so much money? She remembered him as a jolly, rather plump man with a good-humored face, a man who was always making other people laugh and who already had laugh lines around his mouth and his eyes. Not a glamorous person but a good, solid man with a sunny nature. Surely Norman couldn't be involved in the treachery at the Markham Company.

The day was bright, the sky the deep, brilliant blue of October. At last Page drew a long breath. She couldn't cower indoors. She wasn't going to cower indoors. Back in her room she picked up the jade pendant. What could she do with it? For the first time it occurred to her to wonder how the person who had broken into the house yesterday had known which room was hers.

Back in the small sitting room she looked around. On the table was an ancient leather volume which had had the pages removed and had been turned into a cigarette box. She emptied the cigarettes into a cloisonné box, put the pendant in the converted box, and thrust it onto a shelf between two other old leather-bound volumes. No one would guess that it was not what it appeared to be.

At last she was ready for the street. She took a long breath and went out of the house, hearing the door close behind her with a tiny thrill of fear. She tried to laugh at herself. Someone from Markham would be looking out for her, protecting her. There was nothing to be afraid of. Nonetheless, she admitted to herself that she was afraid.

She walked briskly, growing more self-confident, less

afraid, with every step. At Fifth Avenue she turned south, heading for Washington Square and Greenwich Village. Marta lived on Fourth Street. Page had no plan in mind, but something in Mrs. Wentley's anguish made her feel that she should at least make the attempt to meet and persuade Marta to go home.

She went through the Washington Square Arch. A few children were playing in the square; she laughed as a ball nearly struck her, and she tossed it back to a small boy, who seemed to be afraid that she would pocket it.

A girl sitting on a bench watched her somberly. She wore tight blue jeans, a tight sweater, dark hair hung straight and limp over her shoulders. Her face was gaunt, her big eyes defiant. Just another hippie, Page thought, but there was something disconsolate about the girl's expression and posture that hurt her. Leslie had always laughed at her because she seemed to feel other people's hurts as much as they did.

"You need to grow a thicker skin," she had said once, affectionately.

What Page longed to say to this forlorn girl was, "You are denying your own youth and charm and femininity in order to defy society. It's easy to see what you are against: all the rules of the world in which you grew up, all its values, all its disciplines. But what are you for? You can't even pride yourself on being different. All you hippies are as alike as two peas in a pod."

Page went past the lonely girl, seeking for Marta Wentley's apartment. The address on Fourth Street was, as Aunt Jane had warned her, a rundown tenement, little more than a slum. Page wondered whether Aunt Jane had been satisfied with the private detective's report or whether she had come, as Page was coming today, to see for herself where and how the girl lived, to try to bring her back home.

There were screaming children in the street, playing baseball to the hazard of their lives, darting in and out among trucks. A couple of long-haired boys, wearing beards that, with their childish features, made them look about fifteen, swaggered down the street, pausing to look at Page with insolent eyes. One of them, after a muttered exchange with the other, turned back, tried to snatch at her arm.

As though emerging out of nowhere, a young man stopped him, spoke a few words in a low voice, and the boy, with a shrug and a blustering attempt at a rude laugh that did not quite come off, went on with his companion. Page looked at the unobtrusive young man and realized that it was the one who had identified himself to Vance in the hotel lobby. She smiled her thanks and entered the building, knowing that while he was close behind, she could be in no danger.

In the narrow, dingy entrance there were mailboxes and cards. "Mary Smith" was the name Marta had taken. Page rang the bell under her card over and over. Then she gave up and walked away. She would try again another day.

As she came back through Washington Square she noticed that the desolate hippie girl was no longer there. She saw the big soaring apartments to the east and west of the square, with their look of luxury. Where but in New York, she wondered, could one find such terrific contrasts within a few blocks? As she turned toward Fifth Avenue a young man emerged from under the canopy of one of the big apartment buildings and walked toward a taxi in which a woman was waiting. For a moment she thought it was Jerry, though she had not seen his face. Still, she remembered, it is often by a characteristic walk that one recognizes people long before one can make out their features. She looked thoughtfully after the cab as it turned a corner. It couldn't be Jerry, of course.

On Fifth Avenue she started to signal to a bus and then recalled the check she had cashed and the bills still untouched in her billfold. She called a cab and gave the address of Alice Harvest.

The building, which Leslie had vaguely mentioned as near Riverside Drive and rather far uptown, was in a neighborhood that had seen better days. It was like a woman wearing a worn suit with so much dignity that she appears well dressed. The little residence hotel was shabby, inexpensive, but reasonably comfortable. Page inquired at the desk for Alice, expecting that she would be asked to go up. Instead, the clerk told Page that Mrs. Harvest would join her in the lobby in a few minutes.

"Page! What a wonderful surprise. What are you doing here?" Alice Harvest embraced her friend exuberantly and then looked around in distaste. "There are a couple of chairs over here. It isn't very private," she apologized, "but it's more comfortable than my room, which is about the size of a shoebox and has only one chair."

Remembering Alice's charming and spacious apartment in San Francisco with its view from the top of a hill out over the bay, Page was puzzled.

"The question," she said gaily, "is what you are doing here."

Alice Harvest was small and fair and pretty. At the mo-

ment she felt aggrieved and her voice was a trifle shrill.
"Well, you know how Ted is. The industrious apprentice.
He works five days a week, and about three nights a week
he brings work home with him so he won't even talk to me,
and lately he's even been spending weekends working on
some big important job."

She added with annoyance, "Too big to explain to my
simple mind, apparently, or he thinks I am too stupid to understand. I told him we hadn't been anywhere since our
honeymoon over a year ago and he said — oh, you know
how easygoing he is — 'Just wait another six weeks, honey,
and we'll have a real vacation.' Six weeks! Well, I ask you.
So I just packed up and came on to New York by myself.
Of course, after the first week I couldn't afford a hotel —
the prices they charge! — so I moved into this place for a
while."

Page looked at her friend thoughtfully, but there was a
twinkle lurking in the depth of the dark blue eyes. "Having
fun?" she asked casually.

"Well, there's not much you can do by yourself," Alice
said fretfully, and Page laughed outright. "It's all right for
you to laugh. You don't have to share a man with his job."

Alice broke off, looking contrite and shocked by her own
lack of tact. "Page! Darling Page. Forgive me. That was a
terrible thing to say. I ought to be whipped for hurting
you like that."

"It doesn't matter," Page assured her. "And you haven't
hurt me. Jerry is out of my life completely. In fact, I'm engaged to marry another man."

"How wonderful! So that's why you look like a different
person. I've never seen you so glowing. Where did you meet

him? Tell me all about it." In her genuine affection for her friend, and real delight in her happiness, Alice put aside her own grievances.

"He is with Markham too," Page said. "He's with the New York office, but he comes out to San Francisco quite often and that is how we met."

All that was true, but Page hated deceiving one of her oldest friends. She removed her glove and showed Alice her engagement ring.

"Beautiful!" Alice said. "And different. Though I must say I prefer diamonds. Somehow people expect diamonds for engagement rings."

"Vance knows how much I love jade."

"Vance! Don't tell me you are going to marry Vance Cooper, the big rising star at Markham's!"

"That's the one," Page said gaily.

"But why on earth have you kept it such a secret? Oh, I suppose you told Leslie. You and Leslie have always been like sisters."

"By the way," Page said, trying to change the subject before she got too involved, "did you know Leslie gave me a most marvelous jade figurine? A museum piece."

"Well, of course, she can afford it. The Trevors are simply rolling in money. Gordon Trevor is always free to spend as much time as he likes going places with Leslie."

Hearing the discontent in her own voice, Alice said, "But tell me about Mr. Cooper and what brought you to New York."

"Vance had to come back, and he asked me to stay with his aunt while I get my trousseau. I didn't have anything but mourning, you know."

"How well I know," Alice said so feelingly that Page laughed.

"Was it that bad?"

"It wasn't good. I suppose he is giving you a terrific whirl. All the gaiety of the big town."

Page groped her way cautiously. She did not want to make a mistake. "Well, of course, I see Vance whenever he is free and can spare the time, but at this point the Markham people are engaged in a terribly important project, something to do with the space race, and perhaps even the future of our country's prestige. It's so hush-hush that Vance couldn't dream of telling me about it. And he is working like mad, just as all the engineers are. But there will be only a few more weeks, and then he will be free to go back to a normal life and have some leisure."

"Don't you mind?" Alice asked. "Being engaged, you have a right to expect a man to pay you a lot of attention."

"I think personal 'rights' have to give way to the big things," Page said. "I wouldn't have as high a regard for Vance as I have if he were willing to drop everything just to play around and amuse me. Anyhow, he simply couldn't do it! Everyone is pushing at top speed. When Vance has finished a day's work," and Page glanced slyly at Alice, "about all he is fit for is a good dinner and some rest. And by that time he has certainly earned it."

For a moment Alice's expression was suspicious, but Page's guileless face did not reveal her thoughts.

"The engineers at Markham Electronics aren't all that dedicated," Alice said at last. "Some of them have time for a personal life and a little fun. Take Norman Graham, for instance. Did you know Helen broke her engagement to him?"

Page nodded.

"I called Norman when I got to New York, and he's been taking me out now and then. There's no harm in it," Alice added hastily. "Ted wouldn't mind. Actually the only reason Norman asks me to dinner is to get a chance to talk about Helen." The look of discontent was back on her face. "I don't know what Helen wants. Norman is as nice a man as you could ask for, and he gives you the best. Dinner at the most expensive places and a Cadillac to take you around. What more could she want?"

"Norman didn't inherit money, did he?" Page asked casually.

"Good heavens, no. His parents own a little hardware store in a small midwestern town where they both still work. Norman went through college on scholarships. Say, what are you getting at, anyhow?"

"I was wondering how he manages to be such a free spender."

"That's funny. Helen wondered about that too. She said something about a man named Micawber. I didn't know who she was talking about. Does he work for the company?"

As Page burst into a gale of laughter Alice demanded, "What's so funny?"

"Alice, you mean to say you've never read *David Copperfield?*" When Alice shook her head, Page went on, "That novel is filled with the most unforgettable characters. One of the most marvelous is the improvident Micawber who said: 'Annual income twenty pounds, annual expenditure nineteen six, result happiness. Annual income twenty pounds, annual expenditure twenty pounds ought and six, result misery.' "

"I suppose that's true," Alice admitted reluctantly. "Ted insists on saving something every month. When I think of all the things I'd like to have I get so mad at him!" After a moment's thought she added, "I guess you think I've been unfair to Ted, that I ought to have stayed home to look after him and make him more comfortable."

"Oh, I'm sure he is fine," Page said cheerfully. "I was talking to Leslie over the telephone just this morning. That's how I got your address. She said she had asked Ted to dinner one night last week because he was sick of his own cooking. But she didn't say anything to indicate that he isn't looking well or anything like that."

"She wouldn't know," Alice said so sharply that Page had to drop her gloves on the floor and bend over to conceal her face and hide her amusement. "Ted never complains. And he gets just terrible sore throats and never does anything about them unless someone keeps at him."

Page glanced at her watch. "I must run!" she exclaimed. "But I'll call you in a few days and let's arrange to have lunch. I'd like you to know Vance's Aunt Jane even if Vance is too busy to join us."

"Well —" Alice hesitated. "That would be fine. But, Page, I'm thinking of going back to San Francisco. I hate flying, but I think I'll fly back. You can get there so much quicker."

Page's taxi driver wondered what amused the pretty girl who kept laughing to herself all the way home. Until, that is, he said rather sharply, "Anything wrong, lady?"

She raised a startled face. "No. Why?"

"Car seems to be tailing us. I kind of wondered if you were in some sort of trouble."

"Of course not," she assured him.

When the taxi drew up at the Murray Hill house there was no other vehicle in sight. Nevertheless, Page paid the driver before she got out and then scurried quickly from the curb to the door.

Looking after her, the driver noticed the house she had entered. That night he told his wife, "I just thought I'd keep it in mind in case something happens. It looked like trouble to me. Real trouble. Not just a guy following a pretty dame. I saw her face when she ran for the door. In spite of what she told me she was plenty scared."

ELEVEN

THAT NIGHT Vance worked late and did not return until after Page had gone to bed. She and Aunt Jane dined alone and later talked in the little upstairs sitting room. Page made no reference to her abortive attempt to find Marta. Until, or if, she could accomplish something, she would only cause pain by mentioning the missing girl or appear to be asking for Mrs. Wentley's gratitude before she had done anything to earn it.

Mrs. Wentley, in a long, black lace dinner dress, wearing a diamond necklace, was a stately figure. If Page had been meeting her for the first time she would have been somewhat overawed. Instead, she found herself gently led on by the older woman to talk about her father, about their life together in Peru, revealing, without stressing, the extent of their companionship and mutual devotion.

For the first time she really wanted to talk about Jerry, to tell this kindly woman of the pain and humiliation of her broken engagement. But she was stopped by the fear that Mrs. Wentley would believe she had become engaged to Vance as a kind of rebound, that a girl who had been cast off by one man would have no particular value to another.

Instead, she talked about her job with the Markham Electronics Company and her experiences as a working girl.

"I often wish," Aunt Jane said, "that girls had been allowed to work in my day. It is a good preparation for life, even if they don't need the money, and today most families need to have two incomes. But when I was a girl, the only acceptable job was that of schoolteacher, except for the very poor. It seems to me that only by working in a shop or a factory, in an office or at a profession, can a girl possibly understand the conditions under which the man she marries has to work. If she knew how hard it is to earn a living she would be more careful with his money; she would not expect the impossible of her husband."

She broke off, a faint flush on her cheeks. "You must think me absurd, my dear. I who have failed so badly with my daughter to suggest what other girls ought to do."

"It's hard to tell, sometimes, whether one has failed or succeeded. Perhaps Marta is learning that there are worse problems than her own. As soon as anyone learns that, I think he is on the way to coping with his own, don't you? He can see them in better perspective." Page laughed. "Someone said that, no matter how sorry we feel for ourselves, if we had to exchange our troubles for those of someone else, we'd stick to our own."

Without waiting for a comment, she asked about the meeting of the League of Women Voters.

"I believe every woman should be an informed citizen as well as be trained to handle money and earn it," Aunt Jane said. "Women struggled hard to get the vote, to have equality with men. Now they ought to make sure they understand the issues, know about their candidates, and carry out their duties as citizens. I have no patience with the women who complain about their schools and then don't bother to find out what makes them inadequate and do something about it."

The telephone gave a muted ring and, with a murmured excuse, she answered it.

"Yes? . . . Oh, yes, Beverly . . . I hope they are making you comfortable at the Beekman . . . Good . . . Of course, I'll be happy to see you. Just let me check my calendar . . . Yes, come then. I'll be quite at leisure."

When she had set down the telephone she looked thoughtfully at it for a moment. Then she said slowly, "I wonder if I have been unkind to Beverly."

"Unkind to her! According to Vance, you even paid for her education."

"Yes, I did. But I know very little about her; I never asked her to visit me. Only recently have I seen anything of her since she was practically a baby. I'm afraid — that is, apparently she knew from Vance that my daughter has left home. I wonder if I have given her the impression that I intend her to fill that empty place. If so, I have been both misleading and unkind."

"Not you," Page said confidently, but Mrs. Wentley continued to look disturbed. At length Page went to the record player and, after hunting through the record collection, put on a Mozart violin concerto. The evening ended in beauty, although the two women were both so engrossed in their own thoughts that it is unlikely either of them listened to it.

ii

Again there was no note from Vance next morning, but there was a telephone message transcribed by Perkins.

"Will Miss Wilburn please call Mr. Norman Graham at the Markham Electronics Company at her earliest convenience?"

As soon as she had finished her breakfast Page dialed the number and asked for Norman Graham.

"Graham speaking," he said curtly.

"Norman? This is Page Wilburn."

"Oh, yes. Well, look here, can you lunch with me today? Say twelve-thirty at Sardi's?"

"That would be fine."

"Good. See you then." He broke the connection without further words.

"I'll be having lunch at Sardi's with an old friend," Page told Mrs. Wentley.

"But, my dear, you could have asked her here, you know. I want you to regard this as your own home."

"That's terribly kind but, actually, he probably wouldn't have much time for lunch as he'll have to go back to his office."

"Oh, of course." After a slight pause Mrs. Wentley went downstairs to discuss menus with her cook. Page was aware of a faint chill. She wondered whether Mrs. Wentley thought she was making a practice of seeing other men. Jerry's call the day before had not helped the situation.

The perplexing thing was that Norman Graham should not only know of her presence in New York but know where she was staying.

That was explained within minutes of their meeting at the famous theatrical restaurant. Page had encountered Helen's fiancé only a few times, and all the meetings had occurred since she had worn mourning. She was aware, in some amusement, that he did not recognize her when she spoke to him in the crowded entranceway to Sardi's. Again she wore the gray dress and coat, the jade pendant hung around her neck.

"Page! Well, you are really something," he said, his face beaming. Then the good-humored smile faded as they followed the headwaiter toward the table Norman had reserved.

Norman waited only until the waiter had taken their order and gone to demand, his eyes cold and angry, "What the hell are you trying to do to me, Page?"

She was so astonished by this sudden and unexpected attack that she could only stare at him.

"And don't try to play the innocent," he snarled. "I happen to know better."

"Look here," she said, suddenly as angry as he was, "I haven't the slightest idea what you are talking about. I haven't done anything to you. How could I? Why should I? And how did you know I was in New York and where I was staying?"

"Miles Forrest told me. He's head of my department. He found out yesterday that a security check has been put on me. On me! And why? Because I was one of the people who suggested that you work for Markham. Forrest backs his people and he was burned up about it. So am I. So I ask you, what the hell are you trying to do to me?"

"Not one single thing. You've simply got to believe me."

"You mean that you deny having anything to do with this security check-up? You haven't gone around pointing a finger at me?"

"Mr. Markham asked me how I happened to take a job there."

"And why," asked the angry young man, "would the great Markham be bothering about a little stenographer? Can you figure an answer to that?"

Red spots of anger flamed on Page's cheekbones. "Yes, I

can," she sputtered. "He was an old friend of my father's. I told him that you and Ted Harvest had both said it was a grand place to work. And that's all I said about you."

"Well, well. It begins to look to me as though it's really you they are checking on," Norman said slowly. "That's interesting. And what have you been up to, my pretty one? Whatever it is, you've blossomed like a rose under it."

"I'm engaged to marry Vance Cooper."

Norman Graham's scowl disappeared. "So that's it! Anyone who gets near Cooper practically has to walk through an electric eye. But he's a fine guy. I congratulate you, Page. In fact, I congratulate both of you. I'd tell him personally if I moved on such a lofty level."

"Thank you."

"Cooper is a big improvement on that dope you were tied up to once, that tailor's dummy who was training to look nice at diplomatic dinners, buttering up the ambassadors' wives."

Page made no comment.

Norman's momentary cheerfulness faded again. "Just the same," he said, his face clouding, "I think the Markham people carry things too far when they pry into a man's private life. I'd like to know just how much their attitude toward me had to do with Helen's breaking our engagement. You know that's off, don't you?"

"Leslie mentioned it. And then only yesterday I saw Alice here in New York and she told me about it. I'm terribly sorry."

For a little while they devoted their attention to their lunch. Or at least they appeared to do so. Norman was wondering about the girl across the table from him and she was wondering about him, about the beautifully tailored suit he was wearing, about the Cadillac he had recently bought. Where was the money coming from?

"Apparently," Norman said at last, "the security men seem to think my broken engagement is significant of something or other, though, for the life of me, I can't see how they could tie that up with Markham Electronics." When Page made no comment he said casually, "How long is it since you have seen Helen?"

"Not for a long time."

"Is she — is Helen — have you heard whether she is going to marry anyone else?" he blurted out unexpectedly.

"I don't know," Page said.

"She and Alice have always been close, like you and Leslie. Didn't Alice say anything? Drop any hint? I'd have done anything in the world for Helen, Page. I'm crazy about her. How did I lose her?"

Page broke a hot roll, buttered it, put it back on the plate untasted. "Because you have too much money," she said bluntly.

He stared at her in frank disbelief. "Oh, come on, Page, you'll have to do better than that. I have my salary as an electronics engineer and that is all. I'm not a top man; so far as that goes, I'm pretty near the bottom, as the latest employed. No savings. No stocks. Too much money. Yah!"

"No hidden assets?" she asked.

"No hidden —" He pushed back his plate, and the look on his face was not pleasant at all. "Is that what you've been telling the security boys at Markham's, Page? That I have hidden assets? Too much money!"

"I haven't told them anything, Norman. You'll have to believe me. I'm probably to blame for the check being made on you. I — sort of got tangled in things by accident, so they checked on me. Then they wanted to know who suggested that I work at Markham's, and I told them it had been you and Ted Harvest. That's the second time I've explained my position to you. It's the last time I intend to do so. I am not holding out anything."

"And all this money I'm supposed to have? Where did you get that?"

Page made a little gesture of despair. "That was what Helen was worried about."

His expression was blank. "Helen?"

She nodded.

"Helen thinks I have too much money? That's just plain crazy."

"Well, not exactly that you have too much but that you spend too much."

"But —" The young man's appetite was gone now. He rubbed his hand over his head in bewilderment. Then he leaned forward. "Look here, Page," he said earnestly, "let's clear this up, shall we? Do you know Helen's father?"

"No, I have never met him."

"Well," Norman was more animated now, it was clear he had a deep admiration for the older man, "he is quite a guy. In fact — quite a guy. Big handsome fellow, looking not more than forty-five. Well cared for, sunlamp tan, massage, that sort of thing. Tailormade suits. Drives a Lincoln. In fact," as though he could not improve on the phrase, "quite a guy. So I thought, that's what Helen is used to. That's what she wants. So that's what I'll give her. And that is why —" He broke off. "What on earth are you laughing about?"

"Not laughing," she denied. "Just smiling, and yet it's not a bit funny that such misunderstandings can grow be-

tween people. The truth is that Helen always hated and resented her father's extravagance; it prevented her and her
mother from having even necessary things or the security
of knowing the household bills were paid. She would have
been happier with a Ford or even a Volkswagen —"

"Well, darn it, so would I!"

"Then tell her so, Norman," Page said. "And if anyone
in the security branch asks you about all that money you
have been throwing about, tell them the truth. Someone
may get a laugh out of it but that doesn't really matter, does
it?"

"They can laugh their heads off. And if things work out
I'll buy you a diamond necklace." Norman broke off again
as Page began to laugh. This time they laughed together.

iii

"I just heard the tail end of it when I managed to pass
their table," the security agent said. "Sardi's is so crowded
these days you need a shoehorn to get through. They sat
there, the best of friends, laughing their heads off. All I
heard him say was that if things worked out he was going
to buy her a diamond necklace."

The department head avoided looking at Vance Cooper.
Tough on the guy. He had been forced by Markham into
this ridiculous situation with the girl, found out that she
had been mistaken for the foreign courier — or had she?
— and then fallen in love with her. A blind man could see
what had happened there. Even if he had not been so furious
about their using the girl and the jade pendant to lure the
enemy, it would have been clear that he was nuts about
her.

Now it began to look as though she were involved in Op-

eration Homebase in an ugly way. No one yet knew who
had planted the ferret-faced man on her trail, but it was
clear now that it was the girl and not Cooper whom the man
was shadowing. An operative had been set following him —
really the thing was becoming ridiculous, a regular proces-
sion with one spy following another this way — but so far
no one had discovered to whom Ferret-Face reported or
how he did it.

And, last of all, the girl had been seen today, lunching
with one of the electronics engineers engaged on Operation
Homebase, in fact with the very man who was under investi-
gation because he had suggested her working for the firm.
Already they had dug up some interesting and significant
facts. Norman Graham seemed to be spending a great deal
of money, and he had been heard offering the girl a diamond necklace for — well, what did he intend to pay for
with that kind of bribe?

Vance was aware of what the men around him were
thinking. There was no point in arguing. The facts would
establish themselves sooner or later, but he hoped it would
be soon. Anything was better than this gnawing suspicion,
this doubt of Page.

No, he told them, he had nothing to add to what had already been told them beyond the fact that Page Wilburn's
room at his aunt's house had been searched, presumably by
someone who had a key, as the locks had not been forced.

"How would anyone know which room she occupied?"

"Probably by her clothes. I don't know."

"And there is nothing more —"

"Oh, there's one thing, but I don't suppose there is anything to it." Vance told them about Jerome Brooks, who
had formerly been engaged to Page, had broken the en-

gagement, and then had taken the same plane to New York and called on her at his aunt's house. Page had wondered what had brought him back into her life and apparently once more eager to marry her. He had lost interest in her when her father lost his money. Now he wanted to be taken back; in fact, he assumed that he would be taken back.

Page's idea, Vance explained, was that Jerry Brooks might conceivably be after the pendant. He had known that both she and Cooper worked for Markham. Who had told him? Her friends had naturally dropped him when he broke the engagement. He had referred to her sudden interest in jade. He wore a signet ring, and the man who had tried to snatch the pendant in Chinatown had worn a ring.

"We'll see what we can dig up on this guy Brooks," one of the men said without much interest. "At least the young lady seems to have a variety of admirers."

TWELVE

". . . AND that's what worried me," Beverly Main said earnestly. "I know how kind you are. How trusting. How generous. Who would know that better than I? When I think of all you have done for me over the years, though I have no real claim on you at all . . ."

Mrs. Wentley made a small gesture of distress in an attempt to stem the tide of thanks and praise.

"Of course, all that counts with a man is a pretty face," Beverly went on, a sharp edge on her voice. "And I'll have to admit the girl is pretty enough, if you like that type."

"I should imagine," Mrs. Wentley said, a faint amusement in her voice, "that anyone would like that type. She is really lovely, and with her bone structure she'll still be beautiful thirty years from now. Vance says people turn to look at her wherever she goes, and yet she's so lacking in vanity she doesn't even seem to notice it."

The words of praise for a rival were bitter to swallow. Beverly bit back the angry retort she wanted to make, intelligent enough to realize that she would only injure herself in the eyes of the older woman, of whom she stood considerably in awe.

"But there are some things which I feel you should know," she persisted.

Mrs. Wentley protested firmly. "My dear, I really cannot listen to gossip about Vance's fiancée. It would be unpardonable in me."

"Not if you are saving him from a terrible disillusionment?" the girl said. "Perhaps even public dishonor?"

She had Mrs. Wentley's full attention now. "I think," the latter said quietly, "that you will have to explain, Beverly, as long as you have implied so much to Page's discredit."

The girl who called herself Beverly Main looked down at her long kid gloves, smoothed them, laid them carefully across her knee, pulled gently at the fingers. Curiously predatory hands the girl had, Mrs. Wentley thought, and was ashamed of herself. It was so fatally easy to say things like that — predatory hands, eyes too close together, weak chin — and try to establish meanings in them. It was almost as bad as saying all Germans are alike, and all Jews, and all Russians, and all Frenchmen. Yet we knew how different Americans could be from each other. It was lazy thinking. She would not permit herself to do it any more.

"What I don't suppose Vance told you," Beverly said, "or rather what I don't suppose he knows, is that this Page Wilburn was once engaged to marry a man named Jerome Brooks."

Mrs. Wentley's eyes flickered. Surely that was the name of the handsome, self-assured young man who had brought Page the beautiful red roses that now scented the drawing room and who had sent her upstairs flushed and upset from their interview.

"He comes from a fine family and he is, I understand, destined for the diplomatic service. Page's father lost everything he had, and Jer — Mr. Brooks had to break the engagement. It was essential for him to have a wife with enough money to act as an effective hostess, of course. Anyhow, the girl was left high and dry. Then she turned up at Markham's and made a play for Vance. Naturally he is quite a catch. I notice she insisted on coming East with him. Apparently she doesn't dare trust him out of her sight."

"Really, Beverly —"

"Please, Mrs. Wentley, let me tell you. This is so vitally important to Vance." She summoned up a heartbroken smile. "I suppose you have guessed that I fell in love with him. So I care a lot about his happiness. Well, as I told you, I saw an ad in the Lost and Found column for that jade figurine she is wearing. I'll swear it is stolen and she has no right to it at all."

"One that resembled it," Mrs. Wentley suggested rather desperately, feeling that the situation was getting out of hand.

"Dear Mrs. Wentley, do you really believe there could be another that resembled it? To me it looked like a very rare piece indeed, a collector's item."

This was so manifestly true that Mrs. Wentley was silenced.

"So I can't help wondering about Page Wilburn," Beverly said. She looked at her watch and got up. "I won't keep you any longer."

Mrs. Wentley made no effort to persuade her goddaughter to prolong her visit. She longed to be alone, to be able to think about the suspicions Beverly had aroused against Vance's beautiful fiancée.

"I hope they are making you comfortable at the hotel."

"Very. It's terribly kind and generous of you to put me

up there. I suppose — with Page right here in the house and engaged to Vance — I'd be wiser for my own peace of mind to go away." Bitterness dripped from the girl's voice.

"That, my dear, must be your own decision," Mrs. Wentley said, and it was apparent that she had no intention of interfering. She escorted the girl down the stairs and returned thoughtfully to sit by the window.

There was no truth in it, she tried to assure herself. Vance had a cool head. Lovely as Page was, he wouldn't have fallen so deeply in love with a girl who was dishonest, who was using him for her own ends. Nonetheless there were certain things she could not set aside disregarded.

According to Beverly, Page was penniless, but she seemed prepared to spend a great deal of money on clothes. She was engaged to Vance and yet she received a visit from the man who, according to Beverly, had jilted her. And there was also the man with whom she had made an engagement for lunch, a man whom, apparently, she preferred to see away from the house. And, besides all that, there was the jade figurine. How had it come into Page's possession? Could that be the reason for her room's having been searched?

Perhaps she ought to tell Beverly's whole story to Vance. But Vance loved Page. What possible good could it do to arouse his distrust? Or worse, she thought, aware of her own selfishness even as she thought it, Vance, like Marta, would resent her interference. He would abandon her as her daughter had done. And then she would have no one. No one at all.

At length she decided to take no precipitate action. She would wait and see.

ii

"If you'll let me out here," Page said, "that will be fine."
When Norman had instructed the taxi driver to draw in at
the curb and had helped her out, she said, "Thanks for the
lunch, Norman, and try not to worry. You're bound to be
proved in the clear."

"Thank God for one thing," he said fervently. "Miles
Forrest is loyal to the men in his department. He'll fight for
us, right down the line. Nice to have seen you, Page. Try to
forgive those things I said. I guess I was pretty steamed
up."

"I guess you were," Page laughed. "But it's all right now.
Good-bye."

After stopping to look in the window of an art gallery
at an Italian Renaissance painting, marveling, as she always did, at the freshness and vividness of the colors, she
went on to the dress shop to which Mrs. Wentley had in-
troduced her.

The saleswoman was busy with two middle-aged women
who were determined to buy styles suitable for teenagers.
She had a welcoming smile for Page.

"Perhaps, Miss Wilburn, you would like a fitting on that
white evening dress. After that I have some lovely things
to show you."

Page nodded and let the fitter lift the white dress over
her head, saw her kneel to pin up the hem. She was so engrossed in her thoughts that she was startled to hear the
fitter say, "Will you turn, please? Not quite so far. There!
I think that is perfect." She sat back on her heels studying
the lines of the skirt.

"It's lovely!" Page exclaimed.

"Even in your wedding dress you'll never be more beautiful than in this," the fitter declared, and Page looked in surprise at her reflection. Beautiful? She had never dared to think of herself in such terms.

Later she selected another evening dress and looked at coats. The prices appalled her, and she began to understand Vance's telling her, "It's not such a whale of a lot of money."

Finally she selected a beautifully tailored black coat. She was not, she decided firmly, going to add a fur coat to the amount of money she was already costing the Markham Electronics Company. She found herself wondering, a trifle wildly, how her expenses would be accounted for in the records. Serving as live bait for the enemy? Pretending to be engaged to Vance Cooper? It became too confusing, and she gave up her speculations and came back to the coat.

Cloth would be good enough for her. Anyhow, she remembered with a feeling that was like pain, she would not need a coat warm enough to withstand a northeastern winter. Before Thanksgiving she would be on her way back to San Francisco and a more temperate climate.

When she finally returned to the house on Murray Hill, she was told that Mrs. Wentley was lying down and was not to be disturbed. She had a severe headache.

The realization that her life in New York must be brief, that midnight must come for Cinderella, the silence of the little house, the memory of her talk with Norman Graham who had been so angry with her until she had explained her position, all depressed Page. To cheer herself she dressed for dinner in a flame-colored dress she had selected at the last minute and that had fitted perfectly. The vivid color lifted her spirits like the sound of a trumpet. She went into the sitting room to deposit the jade pendant in her hiding place. Norman, to the best of her knowledge, had not even noticed it; he had been too absorbed in his own problems and his fancied grievance against her.

She turned from the bookshelves as Mrs. Wentley came in. This evening the older woman's eyes were shadowed.

"I'm so sorry to hear about your headache," Page said.

"Thank you, it's much better. Practically gone." Mrs. Wentley dismissed the subject. "What a charming dress."

"I got it this afternoon. I needed something to raise my spirits," Page said before she thought.

"Oh. Didn't you enjoy your lunch?"

"Not very much." Page picked a book at random from the shelves. "Money can make such a mess of things for people, can't it?"

"Can it?" Vance asked soberly as he came up the stairs. "Please don't wait dinner, Aunt Jane. I'll change and be ready to join you in fifteen minutes. I got held up by a conference." He indicated the briefcase in his hand. "And I'm afraid I'll have to work tonight."

He came to put his hand on Page's shoulder, to tilt back her chin, kiss her lightly under Mrs. Wentley's observant eyes. In spite of herself Page felt her shoulders grow rigid, felt herself draw back from that dutiful kiss, given her so Vance's aunt might not suspect anything was wrong between them.

His eyes narrowed as he felt her withdrawal and he released her at once.

"Of course we'll wait dinner," his aunt said. "And take your time, my dear. You'll have nervous indigestion if you try to rush your meals that way."

Vance laughed at her. "It would take more than that to upset an old workhorse like me, Aunt Jane."

Neither woman spoke while they waited for Vance to change. Something was wrong. Page had felt it from the moment Mrs. Wentley had come out of her room, her eyes shadowed, her manner restrained. Something had changed her attitude toward Page.

When Vance came from his room and escorted them down to dinner, she felt the same change in him. He said very little, but it seemed to Page that he was watching her, as though half expecting to catch her off guard, that he was weighing everything she said as though seeking for some hidden meaning. She wanted to cry out to them both: What is wrong? What are you thinking?

Instead, she sought desperately for ways of breaking the silence that threatened to engulf the little dinner table with its gleaming linen and silver, its soft candlelight.

"That's a stunning dress," Vance said at last. "You should wear bright colors more often."

"That's what Leslie tells me." Page turned to Mrs. Wentley and described the clothes she had seen at the dress shop and what she had purchased.

". . . and a black cloth coat," she concluded.

"You'll need fur," Vance said. "You aren't accustomed to our severe winters."

Then he recollected, as Page had done, that she was not buying clothes for a New York winter, and he fell silent. It was only when he became aware that his aunt was looking from him to Page in growing wonder and anxiety that he broke the uneasy silence by saying casually, "Aunt Jane, how is Beverly making out?"

"I saw her this afternoon. She came down to have tea with me."

"And what did she have to say?" he asked idly, and was surprised to see the look of distress on his aunt's face.

"Why — nothing of importance."

That's what is wrong, Page thought in a moment of insight. Beverly Main has been here; she has said something about me; she has aroused Aunt Jane's distrust.

"Did you ever give her a key to this house?" Vance asked.

"A key! Certainly not. You forget how little I really know her and that she has never been here until quite recently for an occasional weekend."

"That's odd. Unless the front door and your house door were both unlatched, Perkins can't figure out how she got in the other night — the night Page and I arrived from the Coast. He insists that he didn't admit her; that he never saw her except when you rang and he came upstairs."

"Why — I don't understand —"

"Neither do I," Vance said grimly. "But I suggest that you have the locks changed as soon as you can."

Mrs. Wentley was bewildered. "If I understand you, Vance, you don't altogether trust my goddaughter. But I do assure you I've never given her a key to this house."

"Who do have keys?"

"I have one, you have one, Perkins and his wife each have one, Marta — had one. That's all."

As soon as dinner was over Mrs. Wentley excused herself on the plea of a return of her headache and went to her room, leaving them alone.

Page selected a book and started for her own room.

"Where are you going?" Vance asked.

"I thought I'd read in my room and let you work here in peace."

"Don't run away yet," he said. The dark blue eyes swept quickly over his face, but there was nothing to read. "Aunt Jane will begin to wonder why we see so little of each other. It's not the usual pattern of engaged couples, you know."

"Oh, of course."

This time it was he who gave her a searching look, wondering at the chill in her voice. At length he said, "How about your bait?"

"The jade pendant?" She got up to show him the book-box in which she had concealed it. "I can't wear it all the time," she explained, "and apparently it won't be safe in my room. But this seemed to be a good hiding place, particularly on that shelf with the other old books."

"That's a good idea," he said. "Those were just a fraction of my grandfather's library. There are some interesting and rare items there." He added quickly, "Any reaction to the pendant so far?"

"No. Yesterday I saw Alice Harvest, whose husband is in the San Francisco office. I was not wearing it then but I told her Leslie had given it to me and described it. She didn't seem to be at all interested."

"What broke up the Harvest marriage?"

Page laughed softly. "*Nearly* broke it up. Operation Homebase. Alice thought Ted was neglecting her so she came to New York in a huff to have a vacation of her own and assert her independence. And she hates it because nothing is fun for her without Ted. You should have heard the way I talked to her. Like a Dutch uncle."

"Why was that?"

"Because she needed some sense shaken into her. I

said you and I were engaged but, of course, I practically never saw you because the job was so important that everyone was giving it all the time and energy he had. I said I wouldn't think much of you if you were willing to give up everything just to amuse me. And," Page laughed again, "I gave her a pitiful account of Leslie having Ted to dinner in San Francisco because he is practically fading away from neglect, and half starved on his own cooking. So Alice decided she'd better fly back at once. It seems Ted gets worse sore throats than anyone and he doesn't take care of them and he may be getting one this very minute."

Vance's somber face relaxed in a grin. "Machiavellian tactics," he said. "I'm surprised at you."

"Well, at least it worked," she retorted. "And they really are so much in love it's foolish of her to jeopardize everything just for what she regards as her 'rights.' "

"Was she worried about money?" he asked casually.

Page looked at him in surprise. "No. Why? Oh, she sort of resents Ted's insisting on saving a little every month instead of living right up to his income like —" She stopped abruptly, as though regretting she had said as much.

When Vance saw that she was not going on, he asked, "Did you enjoy your lunch today?"

"I had lunch with —"

"Norman Graham."

"How — oh, of course, the company spies told you." This time there was anger in her voice.

"But you have known all along that we would have people watching you for your own protection," Vance reminded her.

"And to find out who wants that jade pendant. And, incidentally, I wore it today and Norman didn't even notice it. I don't think he'd have paid attention if I had been decked out in all the British Crown Jewels. He was simply furious with me."

"Why was that?"

"He blames me because a security check is being made on him, and Mr. Forrest, who is head of his department — oh, of course, you'd know that — told him I was the one who had unleashed the bloodhounds on his trail. And Mr. Forrest is angry, too, because he backs his men. And I'll tell you this, Vance Cooper, I don't for one single minute believe that Norman Graham has anything to do with the attempt to steal any high-secret stuff and send it out of the country."

"No one has brought any charges against him — so far." Vance tried to keep his voice level, his eyes raking her flushed face. "You seem to feel rather heated about the way Graham is being treated."

"Well, I hate being put in the position of causing trouble for a friend of mine. So far as I can see, the only sin he's guilty of is ever having had the misfortune to meet me."

The telephone rang and Vance stretched out an arm to pick it up. "Don't go," he said, as Page got up and started toward her room. "I want to talk to you."

He spoke into the telephone. "Yes? . . . Oh, good evening, Ruth . . . Why yes, she's right here." He held out the telephone to Page, his lips shaping the words, "Ruth Forrest."

"Good evening, Mrs. Forrest."

"My dear, this is terribly short notice, but could you and Vance dine with us tomorrow at eight? What with Miles working like a beaver and me in the middle of the season, with engagements simply piling up, this is the best I can do for weeks. But we both want to know you better, for your own sake as well as Vance's."

"That's very kind. I do hope it will be possible. I'll have to find out what Vance's plans are." Page covered the phone and repeated Mrs. Forrest's invitation. At his emphatic nod, she said, "Vance will be delighted. Thank you so much, Mrs. Forrest. We'll see you tomorrow at eight then."

"Fine. Black tie. Miles will be jubilant. Vance is one of his favorite people." There was an odd sound in her voice and Page set down the telephone, frowning.

"What's wrong?" Vance asked.

"Mrs. Forrest certainly doesn't like me."

Light from the table lamp fell on Vance's dark red hair, on the clean, hard lines of his face, on the eyes that were veiled as he looked at Page. Only a moment before he had urged her to stay and talk to him. Now he reached for his briefcase, dismissing her with a murmured, "Good night."

By the time the door had closed behind her he set down the briefcase, reached for the telephone, dialed a number. For a long time he spoke as quietly as he could into the telephone.

THIRTEEN

ALTHOUGH she had chosen a light and entertaining novel, Page found that she could not concentrate on it. Finally she gave up, realizing that she had reread a page at least three times without understanding a single word.

She switched out the bedside light, but she could not sleep. The day had been filled with unpleasant moments. There had been Norman Graham's angry attack on her for setting the security men on his track. Then Aunt Jane had withdrawn from her. That must be the work of Beverly Main. But what did the girl have to gain now that Page was actually established as a guest in the house and her engagement to Vance was recognized by his aunt?

It must be the jade pendant, of course, the one she had practically accused Page of acquiring dishonestly. But how had she known that the pendant would be in Page's possession? One thing was sure: she had recognized it the moment she set eyes on it.

Was it Beverly Main who had searched her room? Apparently Vance believed that, in some way, she had acquired a key to his aunt's house. Page could not repress a feeling of sheer pleasure at the knowledge that Vance distrusted Beverly. Though I have no right, she reminded herself, to care what his opinion of other girls may be — no right at all.

She tried to put Vance out of her thoughts, but it could not be done. He had come home tonight distrusting her because the security people had reported that she had lunched with Norman. He knew, as well as she did, that Miles Forrest's wife disliked her. But why? Why? The only reason she could imagine was that Miles had told his wife Page had set the security men checking on his department and he was loyally defending his staff. But then why had Mrs. Forrest insisted that she and Vance dine with them the following evening?

It was very late when she heard Vance crossing the sitting room toward his own bedroom. He moved heavily as though he were tired. His door closed. At least, Page thought, he has stopped work for the night. He can rest. And with that she was able to rest too. She turned on her side and slept.

That night, while Page slept soundly, the wind rose, cold and fierce, making its bold declaration that summer was gone. Farther north autumn leaves fell in a shower of crimson and gold, bronze and scarlet, making a Persian carpet of the ground, and already trees that had been a miracle of color were stark against the sky.

As a sudden gust of wind lifted the papers on a desk and scattered them, the ferret-faced man leaped to close the window and returned to the telephone in his hotel room and made his nightly report.

The man at the other end of the line listened intently. At length he said, "All right, just keep at it. Fantastically bad luck, of course, but you can't always have the breaks . . . What's that? *You're* being tailed! . . . Who? . . . Well, I'll be damned!" Unexpectedly he laughed.

"Need any extra help? . . . You have someone? . . .

Reliable? . . . Yes, I know but . . . Well, don't lose the girl, whatever you do. She's bad news in four different languages, in my opinion."

The wind rattled the window in Norman Graham's room and he shivered, wishing the heat were not turned down in apartment buildings at night. He pulled on a warm sweater and went back to his desk and the bills stacked on it. Once more he added up the total, staring at it incredulously. How had he got himself into this kind of bind? And how, which was more to the point, was he going to get out of it?

Once more he picked up the receipted bill for a mink jacket, which he had set aside. For a long time he stared at it. I could kill Page for this, he thought. She's responsible.

The wind blew a canvas chair across the roof garden of the penthouse and Miles Forrest ran out to fold it and lay it flat on the floor. He came back to bolt the French windows behind him. For a moment he stood looking out at the towers of lower Manhattan. They never failed to excite him. Men had done this. Men could do anything! Then, hearing his wife's sobs, he turned back with a sigh.

"It's all right, honey," he said soothingly. "Nothing to make such a fuss about."

"I'd never have asked them," she sobbed, "but I thought you liked the girl! I thought — when you were in San Francisco this last time —"

He lifted her chin, bent to wipe her eyes gently, to kiss her lips not so gently. "Did you?" he asked, the ghost of a laugh in his voice.

"And you aren't angry?" Her arms clasped around his neck.

"With you, Ruth? Of course not. And I do like the girl, though you are quite wrong about my knowing anything about her in San Francisco, beyond bumping into her quite accidentally in Chinatown. What I don't like is that she is making trouble for one of my men, and I won't stand for that."

"Well, I can say I'm ill — or something —"

"Nonsense, we'll have them to dinner. Make a thing of it. Anyhow, Vance is a wonderful guy."

"Then everything is all right?"

"Everything is all right," he assured her.

Out on the roof garden a heavy potted plant fell from the parapet to the tiled floor with a crash.

Mrs. Forrest started. "What a horrible wind!"

"What a horrible night," he agreed.

ii

The morning was clear and cool, with the sharp bite of autumn in the air and the sun warm, to remind winter it could not yet have things all its own way. A flawless day after the turbulent night.

Once more Page walked down to Washington Square and through the Arch to Fourth Street. At the dingy tenement building she pressed the bell marked "Mary Smith." Pressed it again.

The inner door clicked open and she went inside, hesitating in the dimly lit hallway with its steep flight of uncarpeted stairs, the air reeking of stale tobacco smoke and yesterday's fried fish.

A girl's voice called down the stairs, "What do you want?"

"I'd like to see you, if I may," Page called back.

"I'm not in the market for anything."

Page laughed. "I'm not selling anything," she called up the stairs, feeling rather ridiculous, with every person in the house hearing the shouted conversation.

"Well," the girl hesitated, "I'm just going out. If it's worth climbing two flights of stairs, come on up."

Page went up. The stairs were very steep and the flights seemed very long. She was breathless when she reached the third floor. A girl stood in an open doorway looking at her. Page recognized her at once as the hippie from Washington Square. It seemed incredible that this should be Marta Wentley, Aunt Jane's beloved and cherished daughter, brought up in a world of dignity and comfort and beauty.

"Well?" the girl demanded, an edge of hostility on her voice.

Seen close up, she looked too thin, almost haggard. But there was something in her face Page had not seen the day before, a kind of glow, as though some inner happiness had set her alight.

"You are Marta Wentley, aren't you?"

The girl caught her breath. Then she said stiffly, "You've made a mistake. My name is Mary Smith." She stepped back inside the room.

Before she could close the door, Page reached it. "Please, Marta! Please don't shut me out."

"Who sent you here?" the girl's face was stiff with suspicion.

"No one. It was my own idea."

"It wasn't such a good idea. You may want to talk to me but I don't want to talk to you."

As Page stepped forward, the girl retreated further into the room. Page followed her and closed the door.

The room was even smaller than the one she had found so cramped in San Francisco; in addition, this one was dark, it was dirty, the noises from the street seemed to blast through the thin walls, the rumble of trucks shook them, the screams of children sounded as though they were inside.

"Well," the girl said at last, trying to sound tough, sounding only rather defiant and pathetic, "have you satisfied your curiosity?" She laughed mockingly. "Don't you like the way I live?"

"Do you like it? It certainly isn't as nice as the room your mother planned for you, is it?" Page said gently.

"How do you know? I suppose my mother tracked me down. It's the kind of thing she would do."

"It's the kind of thing any mother would do when an eighteen-year-old daughter disappeared without a trace. She was frantic, of course. You can probably imagine as well as I can all the terrible thoughts she had, the pictures of you being killed or kidnapped or injured or some awful thing happening to you. The calls to the police and hospitals and — the morgue. It must have been a lot worse than the pain she suffered when you were born, Marta. That was something she welcomed because she wanted you. This was something she thought she had brought on herself by failing as a mother."

There was a startled expression on the girl's face. It occurred to Page that Marta was essentially unimaginative. Completely absorbed in herself and her own feelings, she had probably never even considered what her mother's reaction to her disappearance would be beyond a casual and indifferent "It serves her right."

Marta tried to laugh. "You're quite dramatic, aren't you?"

"I'm just so terribly sorry for your mother I had to try to do something."

"If you think I am going back to be ordered around, told what to do, how to dress, all that jazz —"

"She doesn't expect anything of you. I can tell you this, Marta. I don't think she would ever again in her whole life try to make even a suggestion to you. All she wants is to have you safe and happy. If you could come back to her, that would be heaven. But she isn't thinking of herself, Marta. She is thinking only of you."

"Then she has changed a lot," the girl said, her voice sulky. Something about her visitor put her on the defensive, though she would not admit to herself how keenly aware she was of the contrast between Page's well-groomed beauty and her own sloppy, neglected person.

"She hasn't changed. The trouble is that you are a spoiled brat, Marta, and you never knew what she was like. You thought you were too smart to need any advice. And you know what? I don't think you are smart at all."

"Who do you think you are — talking to me like that?" Marta broke off with a kind of gasp as somewhere close by something metallic fell to the floor. Page's eyes swept around the little room, saw the small closet with a curtain drawn across it, saw a faint movement as though wind had stirred the curtain, though there was no window open. Someone was hiding there, listening to their conversation.

Page turned away. "That's all I came to say, Marta, that you are breaking your mother's heart. How long and how deeply do you think she ought to be punished for doing the best she knew how for you?"

"But what would happen to you if I came back?" Marta asked. "You have my room now, haven't you?"

"If you know that," Page said, "you must be the one who searched the room. You still have a key to the house, haven't you?"

Marta glanced at the curtain, shook her head. "No, I lost it a long time ago."

"That's not true. If you haven't used it yourself you have given it to someone else to enter your mother's house."

"Why should you mind?" Marta said, unexpectedly taking the offensive. "What are you afraid of? Is there something you want to hide?" The big, shadowed eyes looked greedily at the jade pendant.

"Have you?" Once more Page seized the initiative. At first glance she had known that Marta could not be won over by sympathy; she had built too hard a shell of resentment and suspicion. Or, to change the metaphor, the place had to be taken by assault and not by reason. Marta was not a reasonable person. And she was, Page suspected, unusually suggestible. She looked like the kind of person who would respond quickly to any suggestion, to hypnotism.

"I don't know what you mean." Marta edged closer to the closet, as though expecting guidance from the person who hid behind the curtain. "And, what's more, I don't care. You come here, interfering. What's it got to do with you? You don't know what it is to have someone try to run you, to run everything for you."

"I must say," Page remarked candidly, "that I can't see that you've made much of an improvement. Look at the way you live! And you don't even try to earn your way; you just drift, letting someone else's money take care of you. How long since you've looked in a mirror? You may have been pretty once but right now —"

Marta's pink tongue licked out like a cat's. "My, my!" she said softly. "Aren't we superior! And how long, Miss Page Wilburn, do you expect to hold my cousin Vance? You don't have much luck with men, do you?" She laughed. "Until you've really got him hooked and married, don't try to tell me what I've been missing."

Anger raged along Page's veins. She longed to tell the girl what she thought. Then she remembered that Aunt Jane loved Marta; she remembered how disconsolate the girl had appeared, sitting alone in Washington Square. Whatever she was doing, whatever she knew about what went on in her mother's house, Page had to protect her if she could.

"Your room is waiting for you now as it has always been. Your mother has been worrying about that goddaughter of hers who wants to move in on her. She is afraid that Beverly might believe she could fill your empty place there. But no one can do that, Marta; no one in the world."

Page turned and opened the door. For a long moment she hesitated. Then she said, slowly and clearly, loud enough so there would be no possibility of her words not being heard by the person who lurked behind the curtain, "Marta, I'm going now. I want to tell you one thing. Whatever grievances you had against your mother belong five years in the past. It's today that you are supposed to live."

"At least I'm choosing my own life!" Marta snapped.

"Are you?" Page said sadly. "All the evidence makes it

clear to me that you aren't choosing anything. You are being used, Marta, and used, I suspect, for an ugly purpose. One you'd be heartily ashamed of."

She went out and closed the door behind her. She heard Marta's eager whisper, knew someone must have shoved an angry hand over her mouth because the sound stopped so abruptly. Then she walked down the stairs, her heels sounding on each step.

Slowly she retraced her steps, wondering who had hidden in Marta's closet, who controlled her speech and her actions as though she were a marionette. *You are being used.* Well, she had tried to warn her. But was it enough? Or was it too late?

iii

"You think you are being used. That's what you are telling me?"

Norman Graham, a very angry and very alarmed young man, sat at the desk of the head of the security department who was examining a receipt for a mink jacket.

"Let me get this clear," the security man said. "You were going through your personal accounts, because you were beginning to worry about where you stood financially. Under your desk blotter you found this interesting little item." His lips puckered in a whistle. "Seven thousand, five hundred. Must be a nice piece of fur for a small jacket."

"I wouldn't know. I never saw the damned thing." Norman's voice rose to an angry shout. He ran a hand through his hair. "Look here, I can't figure this out. All of a sudden, out of a clear sky, Forrest comes in, boiling with rage, to tell me that I'm being given a check-up to end check-ups. The word has gone out that I'm spending money I have no

right to. I'm too extravagant. I must have hidden assets
somewhere. So I get to work on my bills — all right, I've
been spending too much. I'm willing to grant that. But,
damn it, I haven't any assets; all I have is debts."

The security man gave a sudden blast of laughter, leaning far back in his chair. Slowly a reluctant grin appeared
on Norman's face. "It must sound funnier to you than it
does to me. But what really got me scared was finding this
receipt for the mink jacket. I swear to God I never bought
a piece of mink in my whole life! Someone is having fun and
games at my expense. I don't care how crazy it sounds. I'm
not trying to protect myself. All I say is that the receipt was
planted on me; I'm being used, and it makes me mad as
hell."

"And who do you think planted that receipt on you?"

"I don't know. My own guess would be Page Wilburn.
I was certainly mistaken about that girl. I could brain her
for this."

The security man was a placid person who, by a few
simple questions, got the frown off Norman's face and had
him thinking clearly. He asked a series of quick questions,
which Norman answered promptly.

The security man weighed him without appearing to do
so. Apparently the fellow had been a fool, splashing money
around as though it grew on trees. But he wasn't the first,
and he certainly wouldn't be the last. Anyhow, there was no
indication that he had any hidden assets. He seemed per-
plexed, bewildered, and, naturally, indignant that someone
was making use of him.

"Ever hear of a young woman named Kate Willing?"

Norman shook his head.

"Beverly Main?"

Another shake. Then, belatedly, Norman asked, "Who are they?"

"One girl with two names; the one, we suspect, who is wearing the mink jacket for which you have the receipt."

"There's only one girl in the world for whom I'd care to buy mink and she would probably turn it down anyhow; she'd rather settle for the wool with which to knit herself a sweater."

"It sounds as though you have yourself quite a girl."

"I had. She doesn't like heavy spending either."

"What it adds up to," the security man said calmly, "is that you are head over heels in debt and it's going to take you a long time to get out."

"That's right," Norman said glumly. "My girl will never marry me now. Who wants to start married life by paying for dead horses?"

"You say Forrest warned you about this check we've been making on you?"

Norman nodded. "He's a king, that guy. There isn't a man in the department who wouldn't go to bat for him, because he always goes to bat for us."

"How does he account for this check on you?" The security man, busy filling his pipe, did not look across the table at the harassed engineer.

A flood of angry color washed over Norman's face, which normally beamed from a naturally sunny temper. "So far as I can make out, the whole thing goes back to Page Wilburn. It seems her father was an old crony of Markham's. I suppose that's how she met Vance Cooper. Anyhow, anyone who gets within shooting range of Cooper, while Operation Homebase is in the works, has to be cleared these days. I suppose they wanted to know about me when Page

told Markham I was one of the people who recommended
his company as a place to work. Catch me ever lifting a hand
for anyone else again."

"Why?"

"Because it seems fairly clear to me now that she is the
one who started the talk about my spending too much
money. She really took me in for a while."

"What do you know about her?"

"Well, to begin with, what any man would know. She's
a real beauty, the kind who stops traffic. Her father lost his
money and her fiancé, a good-looking rat named Jerome
Brooks, jilted her, left her high and dry. I met her a few
times while she was in mourning for her father. It wasn't
until we had lunch together I realized what a knockout she
is."

"Anything else?" the security man asked.

Norman shook his head. "That's the works."

The security man looked down at his notes. His agent
had reported that this fellow Graham had offered the Wilburn girl a diamond necklace if everything worked out all
right. He hadn't been in any rage with her then; they had
been laughing together like the best of friends. He looked
back at Norman, whose face was now free of tension.
"You're sure you aren't holding back a thing?"

"Not a thing," Norman said clearly.

The security man made a short note, jabbing his pen vi-
ciously into the paper, though his face remained calm and
unrevealing. He picked up the receipt for the mink jacket.

"You willing to go along to the store and have the salesman take a look at you?"

"You bet I will."

"Right now?"

"The sooner the better, so far as I am concerned."

The security man gave him a puzzled look, shrugged, and slipped into his overcoat. "All right. Let's go."

The manager of the famous fur shop looked at the receipt and nodded. "That's ours."

"Can any of your salesmen identify this man?"

One by one, the manager lined them up while the color deepened in Norman's face.

"This feels like being in a police line-up," he muttered, trying to grin.

"That shows," the other replied, without returning the grin, "that you haven't experienced a police line-up — yet."

Norman's grin vanished. The lines around his mouth deepened but not with laughter. This trip hadn't been made in the middle of a busy day for the fun of it.

One of the clerks stepped forward. "I sold that mink jacket," he said. "I remember the transaction very well. My sales book —" He handed it to the manager who looked at it and nodded.

"This sale was made three months ago, I see. How was it paid for?"

"A cashier's check."

"So you have no record of the name of the purchaser."

"None at all."

"To whom was it delivered?"

"The man who purchased it took it away with him."

"Is this the man?"

The salesman looked at Norman in surprise. "Oh, no, sir," he said promptly. "No resemblance at all."

And at last the security man returned Norman's grin. "You can relax," he said. "But don't mention this receipt to anyone, will you? And don't tell anyone, even Forrest, we've cleared you." There was an odd expression on his face.

For the first time Norman's grin was wholehearted. "I don't need to," he said cockily. "Forrest knows I'm in the clear. I told you — he backs his men."

FOURTEEN

THE clinging white dress was as becoming as Page had hoped. More sophisticated than the clothes she usually wore, its deceptively simple lines molded her supple and graceful young body.

When she went out to the sitting room where Mrs. Wentley and Vance were talking while they waited for her, Vance caught his breath. Page waited, but he made no comment on the new dress.

"Do you think I need a bit of color with this?" she asked, her eyes carrying their message.

"The jade pendant? Might be a good idea." Before Mrs. Wentley's surprised eyes he retrieved it from the book-box on the shelf and hung it around Page's neck.

"Page has found herself a private safe for her jewelry," he said lightly.

"What a clever idea." Whatever had bothered Mrs. Wentley she still had not recovered from. "You look dazzling, my dear, as Vance is no doubt waiting to tell you when you are alone. I do hope you have a pleasant evening." She nodded to them and went down to her solitary dinner.

Abruptly Vance said, "No! Not tonight," removed the jade figurine and restored it to its hiding place.

"But why?" she asked in surprise.

"I don't know. A hunch, if you like. A strong feeling that

the pendant should not be on view this evening. I can't explain."

"Whatever you like," she said.

In the taxi that took them to the Forrest apartment Vance said, "We'll have to watch it, you know. Aunt Jane doesn't think we are behaving like an engaged couple. Another slip like that one tonight and Beverly will be worming out of her the fact that we aren't much in love."

Page winced at the words but she managed to say coolly, "What slip?"

"I didn't tell you that you knocked my breath out in that dress, that you are dazzlingly lovely." Unexpectedly, regardless of the driver's amused and interested eyes, Vance's arm went around her shoulder, he bent over her, found her mouth, and kissed her, a long deep kiss. "Just so you'll get accustomed to it in public," he said when he had released her. "These things take a little practice."

"I must say you don't seem to need any," Page commented, trying to match his light tone, though her heart was thudding, her mouth burned with the pressure of his lips.

The Miles Forrests had a duplex penthouse apartment near the East River in the middle fifties. Although it was too chilly to use the terrace, bulbs had been strung around the three sides of the open area, lighting up tubs of trees and bushes. As there was no wind tonight, canvas chairs and tables had been set up to give the illusion that people could sit comfortably out of doors. The French windows onto the terrace were unlocked so that anyone who wished to do so might go out.

From her conversation with Mrs. Forrest, Page had assumed that she and Vance were to be the only guests. Instead, there were six couples, all of them, as Ruth Forrest explained to Page, members of Miles's department.

"At least the men are. The women are mostly wives. Until this wretched job is done, I suppose they are so used to being together they just take it for granted. But I warned Miles I would do something drastic if any of them so much as dare mention Operation Homebase all evening. This is a time for fun and relaxation."

As her other guests had already arrived, Ruth Forrest was free to devote all her attention to Page. She took her down a gracious flight of marble stairs to the lower floor of the duplex and into a bedroom, which, for the evening, had been turned into a woman's cloak room.

"My dear," she said, "you are simply ravishing in that dress."

"I was just admiring yours," Page said truthfully. Ruth Forrest, in black velvet, wearing a necklace of matching pearls, was a stunning woman.

"And that ermine cape —" Mrs. Forrest took it out of the hands of the trim maid to examine it. "Beautiful thing."

"Oh, that isn't mine," Page said. "It belongs to Mrs. Wentley's daughter Marta, but she has been angelic enough to lend it to me." For a moment Page tried to picture the drab little *hippie* wearing this exquisite fur but failed to do it.

Mrs. Forrest gave the jacket back to the maid and remained beside Page, smiling brightly. "How on earth did you manage to make such an impression on Miles in San Francisco? This last trip he wasn't there more than three or four days. You are a fast worker."

By this time the two women were strolling up the stairs to the great living room and the waiting guests.

"He bumped into me," Page said with a laugh. "I had stopped all of a sudden and —"

"That's when I got you that Chinese silk," Miles broke in, coming up to shake hands with Page. "Wonderful stuff. Scarlet and a deep green and luscious gold —"

"But yards and yards of it. Enough to make dresses for a lifetime," his wife said. She laughed, her eyes moving from her husband's face to Page's. "I always get suspicious when a husband buys his wife such lavish gifts. It must be conscience money."

Tonight Miles Forrest was the genial host, his welcome was warm, but Page, aware that his wife was surreptitiously watching them both, felt constrained.

"So here is Vance's little beauty," he said heartily. "I've been watching Vance. He can't take his eyes off you. And there's another old friend of yours here tonight. Norman Graham. Remember him?" This time there was no ignoring the challenge in his pleasant, hearty voice.

"Yes, of course. I saw him yesterday. But he's not an old friend. It's his fiancée who is my old friend. I met him only a few times before he was transferred to the New York office."

"He's in my department," Miles told her. He smiled pleasantly. "All my guests tonight, except for Vance, are men from my department. I take care of my own, Miss Wilburn."

Page felt herself flush at his tone. "That's what Norman told me. In fact, he hero-worships you as much as Vance does. They can't either of them say enough in praise of you."

Miles laughed. "Come meet our other guests." He swept her along with him.

It was obvious to Page almost immediately that the guests were all, with the exception of Miles himself, on a much lower business level than Vance. She wondered why the Forrests had planned this particular party; then she realized that it was Miles Forrest's way of warning her that he backed his men. She didn't know whether to be amused or indignant, but she was getting a little weary of being regarded as Norman Graham's bad angel.

Apparently Norman had had a change of heart since she had seen him at lunch. His eyes were hard and angry when he looked at her.

"A good guy," Miles said to Page about Norman. "Only trouble is that he's a bit extravagant."

"You say that!" his wife exclaimed, laughing.

The groups met, shifted, reformed. Once Page heard Forrest say, a hard edge on his voice, "Look here, Cooper, I think I have a right to know what's being done in my own department. Sheer luck I found out what was going on."

"Oh, please," Mrs. Forrest wailed. "No business tonight. You promised me."

There was a general laugh that indicated the same problem had become familiar to all the guests.

The dinner was served at a table shaped like a halfmoon so that all the guests could face the magnificent view. The food was superlative and the service quiet and effective.

As Vance's fiancée, and consequently escorted by the highest-ranking man present — really, Page thought, business got more and more like the army so far as precedence was concerned — she sat on Miles's right. On his left was the mother of one of the electronics engineers, an unmarried man. After seeing the mother, Page doubted very much that the poor fellow would ever be able to break away from her and marry. She was a woman who had a definite opinion on all subjects and who stated them without a moment's hesitation, asked or unasked. Disagreement she brushed aside as though it had not been spoken.

Before Miles had an opportunity to devote himself to Page, the mother — her name was Matthews but Page thought of her only as That Dreadful Woman — had smoothly taken charge of her host, and Page turned to the man on her other side, a young engineer who brightened when he began to talk to her. Up to then he had apparently been somewhat subdued by the luxury of his surroundings and was ill at ease. With Page smiling and talking casually, he began to relax.

Of all the people at the dinner party they were the only ones who seemed to be enjoying themselves immensely, laughing, joking, talking eagerly about anything that came to mind. They were having such a good time, indeed, that it was a shock for Page to look up in one of those lulls that sometimes occur and find both Vance and her hostess watching her intently. Then Vance, seated at Ruth Forrest's right, turned back to her and resumed his conversation. But somehow the gaiety and the unselfconscious enjoyment Page had been experiencing were dimmed, lost their momentum. She could not regain them.

Beside her, Miles Forrest was attempting valiantly to devote some attention to her as the guest of honor, but That Dreadful Woman had different ideas. She made it impossible for Miles to turn away from her for a moment unless he were to be downright rude. Once he turned to say, "Miss Wilburn, don't you think —" only to be broken in on by the tiresome, tireless, trumpeting voice of the woman demanding, "How long is this thing to go on, Mr. Forrest?"

"What thing?"

"Don't be childish," she snapped, and her son, sitting further down the table, gave her a look of mute appeal which she sternly ignored.

"This Operation Homebase that is working all your men to death."

"I'm not in a position to answer that," Miles said.

"Nonsense. Of course you are. My son says you have a hand in everything. I just want to know how much longer he is going to be working all hours of the day and night —"

"Mother!" the young man protested.

"I don't mean that my son dislikes working. He's — dedicated."

"Mother," he said, his face scarlet.

Page carefully avoided the laughing eyes of the young man beside her.

"What I want to know," That Dreadful Woman demanded, her strident voice dominating the table, making it impossible for anyone to ignore her, "is whether this is really worthwhile. That is, is all this work and money and information going to help this country or our enemies?"

There was a collective gasp. Then accusing eyes turned on the young engineer.

"I insist that my son give me his full confidence," Mrs. Matthews said firmly. "I know — as I suppose you all know — there has been a leak somewhere. There's a traitor in the company. In fact, the traitor may quite likely be sitting at this table right now."

Vance broke in decisively. "Even if your worst fears should be true, no greater harm could be done than for you to discuss the matter as you are doing at this moment."

Mrs. Matthews, who probably had never been criticized in her life, was dumfounded. She was also, mercifully, silenced.

And at last Miles was free to talk to Page. By this time they had reached the salad stage of the meal. Page nibbled at a hot flaky cheese stick and sighed rapturously. "How marvelous! I can't remember when I've had such a wonderful dinner. I must have put on pounds and pounds, but it is worth every ounce."

"I like to see a girl enjoy her food," Miles said. "You look as though nothing ever bothered you."

Page laughed. "Don't you believe it. I'm bothered about all this casual talk of traitors in our midst, as though they could possibly be people we know and like and break bread with."

Miles was amused. "Why? Do you think they have two heads or wear green beards or have something strange about them, like the men from Mars? They are probably, as we discover whenever one of them is uncovered, perfectly ordinary people, like you or me."

"Not ordinary," Page insisted. "An ordinary person does not betray a country like this. I don't mean we have no faults or shortcomings. Of course we have. But we recognize them, we even publicize them, and we try to overcome them. When people carp, they point out only the bad things; they never balance them against the good. But you don't get a true and honest picture unless everything is in it. Don't you agree with me, Mr. Forrest?"

He smiled at her. "You're a very earnest pleader."

"Because it matters very much. To destroy for personal gain or power seems to me to be a monstrous act, and I don't believe monstrous acts are performed by ordinary people."

"In other words, by monsters." Miles Forrest, aware their conversation had taken too serious a turn, was laughing, trying to restore something like gaiety to the dinner table.

Page laughed back at him as the waitress removed her plate, brought finger bowls on glass dessert plates. While she lifted off the finger bowl Page looked to find that again Vance was watching her. Again her interest in the conversation was diminished by that hostile attention. Even the delectable chocolate mousse failed to cheer her.

The dinner party, which apparently had been arranged at the last moment, was badly assorted. To begin with, it ran in age from Vance Cooper's lovely young fiancée to poor Will Matthews's formidable mother. Dancing was not possible. Few of them were bridge players.

Ruth Forrest handled a difficult situation as well as she could, trying valiantly to keep the engineers apart and to prevent any discussion of their work; but to arrange congenial groups seemed to be almost impossible.

She welcomed the suggestion that her guests, none of whom had seen the terrace, have an opportunity to inspect it. In the bedroom on the lower floor Page let the maid slip the ermine cape over her bare shoulders. In the mirror she saw the girl's face and wondered where she had seen it before. With a shock of surprise she recalled it had been in the woman's room of the hotel where she and Vance had danced. That night the girl had been in evening dress, not in a maid's uniform. The girl met her eyes in the mirror, gave her a faint nod and a smile. Then she went to help another woman with her coat.

The guests, in twos and threes, drifted around the three

sides of the terrace, looked out on the panorama of New York, admired the planting, now protected against the coming winter, that next year would be flowerbeds; the fountain, now dry, that would provide a cascade of water in the summer.

By this time Mrs. Matthews, who had recovered her equanimity and regained whatever self-assurance had been temporarily lost, said in loud tones, "I must say I don't mind my son working hard if he can ever afford a place like this. I've been trying to figure out what the rent must be, let alone the cost in salaries for people to run it."

In an attempt to stop her before she said anything unforgivable, the wife of one of the engineers and Vance reached her at the same time, calling her attention rather desperately to the neat gravel paths, the lawn. There was a general move on the part of the other guests to put as much space between them and her as they could. Page went around a corner to the second side of the terrace, where there was a different and equally terrific view, this one over the East River. She exchanged laughing and admiring exclamations with several people whose names she had forgotten.

Unexpectedly there was a light sprinkle of rain and a general exodus from the terrace. Page had gone on, turning a corner, and was now on the third side of the terrace. There was no view from here, though there was space for lounging chairs and tables and umbrellas during the summer. In front there was the wall of the building.

Suddenly aware of the rain on her hair and cheeks, of the fact that she was alone, she started back to rejoin her party. And the lights went off.

For a moment she was bewildered. Then she put out her hand, groping her way. She was against the wall of the building. If she followed it she would come back to the French windows leading into the great living room.

Then, without warning, a hand covered her mouth, she was being dragged toward the parapet. Her clawing hand scraped against the bricks of the low parapet. She was being lifted —

Someone called, half laughingly, half inquiringly, "Are you lost, Miss Wilburn?" She recognized Ruth Forrest's contralto voice. She was dropped suddenly. There was a flurry of motion and she was alone.

"Mrs. Forrest?" Her voice was scarcely more than a whisper.

"Oh, here you are!" Mrs. Forrest exclaimed. "I was afraid you might have lost your way in the dark. I can't imagine what went wrong with the terrace lights. Those in the apartment are all right, thank goodness. Here, give me your hand and I'll lead you back so you won't bump into things."

As she touched Page's hand she exclaimed, "You're freezing. Your hand is like ice. You aren't ill, are you?"

The trip in the dark around the terrace to the lighted living room seemed endless and terrifying to Page. Her heart was racing with panic. It was an unspeakable relief when she was back inside the long room, which also served as dining room and from which the semicircular table had now been removed.

To Page's relief the party was breaking up. After one searching look Vance was at her side, his warm hand under her arm. "What's wrong?" he asked in a whisper.

"Later," she replied.

She summoned up all her control to stand beside him, thanking the Forrests for a delightful evening. Then they went down in the elevator with half the party. There was only one person in the elevator who had not been a dinner guest. That was the man with the ferret face. He was colorless and looked very angry. Though she had been furious with Vance all evening — first because of that provocative kiss, which meant nothing to him and had wrought such havoc with her, and then for his constant watching of her actions, as though, she thought in fury, he half expected her to leave her spoon in her cup or eat with her knife — she found herself clutching at his sleeve, standing very close to him, grateful for his presence.

They did not speak all the way home in the taxi. Only when he had taken the ermine cape from her in Mrs. Wentley's sitting room did he ask, "What happened to you, Page? You came off the terrace looking as though you had seen a ghost."

"Someone," she said, "tried to throw me off the terrace." And then, somehow, she was in his arms, crying out her fear and her bewilderment, and they held her, strong and warm.

FIFTEEN

"IT'S all right," he whispered, his mouth against the soft honey-colored hair. "It's all right. You're safe now. Nothing can hurt you now."

At last she drew away from him, flushed and lovely, half laughing, half crying. "I'm sorry I went to pieces like that, but it was so unexpected — so terrifying — and if Mrs. Forrest hadn't come when she did — even a minute later —"

"Oh, Page! Page darling!" He drew her down on the couch beside him, her hand clasped in his. "Now tell me exactly what happened." He saw that her knuckles were raw and bleeding.

"That's from the brick parapet," she explained. She had not guessed his face could look so ugly, so menacing. "Well, it began to rain and then, all of a sudden, the terrace lights went out. The rest of the people had gone inside and I was alone. I started back and then — someone was there."

She was shaking now and Vance slipped his arm around her shoulders. "He covered my mouth so I couldn't make a sound and dragged me toward the parapet. He was lifting me when Mrs. Forrest called and came around the corner. He dropped me and just — disappeared in the darkness."

"You're sure he wasn't just taking you in his arms? Perhaps going to kiss you?"

"Oh, no! He was — hurting and he dragged me and then — he meant me to go over."

"You looked so — stricken when you came in."

"So would you if someone had just tried to kill you. Only — why, Vance? It's not just the pendant, is it? I wasn't even wearing the pendant tonight. Why else would someone want to injure me?"

There was a strange look on his face. It was as white as hers, but there were glints of steel in his eyes. "I can think of no less than four persons who could easily be your enemy, Page."

"At least," she tried to steady her voice, "we can eliminate Mrs. Forrest. Whether or not she likes me — and she keeps watching me — she saved my life tonight."

"Whose suggestion was it that we all take a look at the terrace? I was the only one who had been there before and that's why I didn't stay out there."

"I don't remember who suggested it. Mrs. Forrest agreed that it would be a good idea, but I think that was mostly because the party was being such a flop. It never really got going."

"She seems to be hipped on that meeting of yours with Miles in Chinatown."

"Well, actually, it wasn't in Chinatown, though that isn't the point. I stopped on the street and he bumped into me and apologized and then asked the way to Chinatown and went on. But for some reason his wife seems to think he fell for me out there, which is nonsense."

"So that's it!" Vance said. "Poor Ruth." His arm had tightened around Page's shoulders. His face was nearly as white as hers had been. Now, indeed, there was a lovely color flushing her cheeks.

"You know," Vance said slowly, "it's just possible that Ruth's jealousy saved your life. Ironic, isn't it?"

"I don't understand," she admitted.

"I suspect that when the lights went out Ruth thought you might be with Miles and she went to look for you."

"Oh, well, whatever the reason, I'm glad she came," Page said fervently. "I never was so frightened in my whole life." She straightened up, reached for the ermine jacket and groped in the pocket for her handkerchief. With it she drew out a small piece of folded paper at which she looked in surprise. She opened it, a puzzled frown between her brows. She read it, read it twice, then a third time. At last she handed it to Vance. "What in the world!" she exclaimed.

"Ask Marta Wentley," read the typewritten note, "how well she knows Jerome Brooks."

"Where did you get this?" Vance asked.

"I just this minute found it."

He read it again, put it in his pocket. "I don't know what it means, but I'm going to find out, for Marta's sake as well as for everyone else who may be involved. Who could have slipped that note into your coat pocket?"

"I suppose you saw the weasel in the elevator with us when we came down from the penthouse. He looked terribly angry."

"No, I didn't see him. For some reason I always seem to miss him. I was so worried about you I didn't notice anyone else. Where did he get on?"

"But don't you remember? The elevator was filled with guests from the party when we left the penthouse, so it didn't stop except on the street floor."

"But how on earth did he manage to get into Forrest's apartment? Buildings like that have doormen on the job all the time and no one is allowed in the elevators without the permission of the tenants."

Page shook her head. "Then there was the maid." She explained about recognizing the girl who had acted as maid for the party but whom she had previously seen in evening dress at the hotel where she and Vance had danced. "She sort of smiled and nodded at me. I wondered if she was one of them."

"Of whom?"

"Our theme song. I wonder who's watching us now. Or do they use women operatives?"

"I have no idea, but I'll find out in the morning. Can you think of anyone else who could have put that note in your pocket?"

"Well, both Mr. and Mrs. Forrest were beside me, of course, when I said good night and shook hands with them. Norman Graham was next to me in the elevator when we went down, but he acted all evening as though he simply hated me and I can't see why he'd be bothering to give me a note when he could speak. Poor Mr. Forrest behaved as though he were trying to save Norman from my clutches or my deadly malice or whatever bad influence I'm supposed to have. It's all rather silly, but it's disagreeable too."

"It's a bit more than that, Page." At something in Vance's voice Page drew away from the shelter of his arms to look up into his face. "What I am telling you now is on my own discretion, against the advice of the whole Markham outfit. Only — I don't think I'm mistaken about you."

"Mistaken?" Page was bewildered. After the shock at the penthouse she wasn't thinking clearly. She shook her head and the soft hair brushed Vance's cheek momentarily.

"Norman Graham," Vance said quietly, "has — had — in his possession a receipt for the mink jacket that Kate Willing is wearing."

"I don't know what you are talking about. Who is Kate Willing?"

"I thought I'd told you. She's the girl who is masquerading as Beverly Main."

"Masquerading! No, you didn't tell me. And your aunt still doesn't know and —"

"Aunt Jane must not know, Page. She would give herself away at once."

"But Norman — Vance, do you mean that Norman is the traitor, that he paid the girl to be the courier to deliver the jade pendant that got into my hands?"

When he made no comment Page said impatiently, "That is absurd. Aside from the fact that he doesn't have that kind of money, he wasn't even interested in the pendant when I wore it at lunch. I told you that." Page looked up to see Vance's eyes, cold and steady.

"What I want to know, Page, is why, if he doesn't have that kind of money, he was offering you a diamond necklace?"

If his arm had not been so close, lying across the back of the couch, he could not have stopped her as she tried to jump up. "Wait!" he said.

Fury blazed like swords in her blue eyes, glowed like fire in her lips. "Let me go!"

"Not until you explain."

"All right, I took this job to be useful. In doing so I brought suspicion on two innocent people: Ted Harvest and Norman Graham. Yes," she rushed on before he could interrupt, "Norman. He asked me to lunch because Mr. Forrest told him he was being investigated as a security risk and he blamed me. I told him I'd mentioned him as recommending Markham's as a nice place to work and that was all. And he said they were prying into his personal life and even wondering about his broken engagement. And I told him," Page almost stuttered in the rush of words, "Helen had been afraid to marry him because he was too extravagant. So he said he was trying to be like her father because he thought that was what she admired. And we agreed he was a fool and he said he was going to reform and he was glad I'd told him and he said — he said if it worked out all right with Helen he'd give me a diamond necklace and then we laughed because it sounded as though he were an incorrigible spendthrift. And that's all. Until tonight. He had changed again and he suspected me and — let me go!"

Vance had pulled her back into his arms, bent over her. "Never," he said.

"I hate you," she whispered.

"Do you, Page? Do you?" His lips touched her forehead, her cheek. "Why?"

She turned her head away. "Because you suspect me of horrible things. And because you kissed me the way you did in the taxi tonight. As though — as though it didn't matter about me at all."

"I fell in love with you before we even got off the plane. Didn't you know that, Page?"

Her head moved against his shoulder.

"Didn't you?" He made her look at him. "Page? Page darling —"

And this time she did not turn away her face.

ii

"But the note you found in the pocket of that jacket," Vance said after a long interval.

Page came back from the dazzling brightness of the future to the uncertain present.

"It could have been anyone, I suppose."

"No, it couldn't," he said coolly.

"What do you mean?" She was surprised by his tone. Her head seemed to have settled comfortably on his shoulder. Now she sat up, staring at him.

"How many people know about Marta? How many people know about your — former association with Brooks? Remember that Marta has been gone for five years and Aunt Jane does not speak of her. Another thing: how would anyone know that you had been informed about Marta?"

"Well, that's something I've been intending to tell you," Page said, "but there just hasn't been an opportunity." She described her two visits to Fourth Street, her interview with Marta on the second occasion and its unsatisfactory outcome.

"You went down to the Village to seek her out and try to persuade her to come home. You've been performing service over and beyond the call of duty, haven't you, darling?"

"She's so pathetic, Vance, though she wouldn't forgive me for saying so. And Aunt Jane is so horribly lonely without her. The queer thing is that Marta is lonely too. And someone is trying to control her. I'm sure of that. There was someone hiding in her closet while I was there, signaling to her what to say and what not to say."

Vance was amused. "Knowing your crusading spirit, I'm surprised you didn't fling open the closet door and confront the lurker."

"It wasn't a door, it was a curtain. And I did try to warn her. I told her she was being used."

"Oh, Page! My darling little fool."

Vance caught her against him, scolding her for taking idiotic chances, for general foolishness. Page, her cheek pressed against his, did not seem in the least offended.

When he released her at last he said, "I'm going to return that jade figurine to the office tomorrow. We're never going to take another chance on you. I'm turning it over to the security division. I'm all for cooperation, but I'm not going to sit back and watch someone throw you off a penthouse twenty stories in the air."

"Vance." Something in her voice made him turn her face so he could see it more clearly. "Before you do anything — anything you can't undo — I'd better tell you several things. Marta knew who I was, she knew I was staying here and occupying her room, she knew I was engaged to marry you, she knew I had been jilted by another man. And," she groped blindly for his hand, "I was wearing the jade pendant and she looked at it as though it required all her will power not to snatch it away from me. Vance," her voice had dropped to a whisper, "I'm sure she knows about the pendant. Otherwise, a girl who had put away all the luxury of her home wouldn't care for a thing like that. It has to be because someone told her the meaning of the figurine, what it contained."

"I see," he said grimly.

"Do you suppose that Jerry really does know her, that he told her? That might account for his queer attitude toward Aunt Jane and you, as though he knew something — uh —"

"To our discredit," he concluded. "There is one thing sure, Page. We must have all the facts, no matter who gets hurt."

"But suppose it is Aunt Jane who gets hurt. She has already been hurt so much."

"Don't you think I would hate that too? But there is more at stake than an individual. If I can get Marta out of the spot she seems to be in without public disgrace I'll do it, but I'm not going to hold back anything from our security branch."

"I understand that," she said, "but I'm sorry." She drew away from the shelter of Vance's arms. Without their warmth she felt chilly. She shivered.

"It's in your hands now. I'm going to bed."

"You're a very gallant girl, Page. I'd never have let you get involved if I had had any idea you would be in danger. Markham will probably have my scalp for this. From now on I won't let you out of my sight. The people who are supposed to be guarding you certainly blundered tonight. They ought to lose their jobs for that."

iii

"If Mrs. Forrest hadn't come around the corner of the terrace when she did, the girl would have gone over," the ferret-faced man said into the telephone.

"You slipped up that time, didn't you?" a grim voice said and the man flushed.

"I slipped up," he agreed quietly. "It won't happen again."

"It had better not, unless you assume the girl has as many lives as a cat. How did you manage to get into the penthouse?"

"When we were tipped off to the party I found that they were going to have the terrace lighted. So I went up with the men who strung the light bulbs, and then stayed. There's a little room for tools and things up there on the roof. I kept out of sight until it was safe to move around. Once people came out on the terrace, of course, I was busy ducking out of the way."

"Too busy to do the job you're paid for," the savage voice said.

"I've admitted that I slipped up. But I don't see who could have handled it better."

"What was Mrs. Forrest's reaction to this attempt on the girl's life?"

"She didn't know. At least — it happened in the dark and the girl didn't tell her out there. The party was breaking up by then. Probably the girl unloaded the story on Cooper on their way home. And now I expect I'll have him gunning for me, too."

"I wouldn't be surprised." The other man was not sympathetic. "Keep me posted."

iv

"The party was a flop, wasn't it?" Mrs. Forrest said. The lights in the living room were out now, and the couple had gone down the stairs to the bedrooms on the lower floor. The extra waiters and the maid hired for the evening had been paid and sent away.

Mrs. Forrest stood before her mirror, wearing a flame-colored negligee, against which her dark hair gleamed. She was a very pretty woman.

Her husband came to bend over and kiss the back of her neck. "I'm a lucky guy," he said. "All these years and I've never got used to the fact that I have a wife like you."

She put down the hairbrush and turned to face him, smiling. "Then you don't mind too much about the party's being so dull."

"It wasn't your fault. I shouldn't have asked that group of people. They are fine when they are working together," he said loyally, "but they didn't fit with Cooper and his fiancée. They are in so much lower a bracket they don't feel at ease with him, though I must say I've never known him to throw his weight around."

"You are out of their bracket too," she reminded him.

He brushed that aside. "Well, we've worked together a long time." He laughed. "The worst part of the evening was that Matthews woman."

"Isn't she awful! I hope her son won't lose his job for being so indiscreet in talking to her."

"We'll have to transfer him to a department where there are no secrets," he said lightly. "He's too good a guy to fire."

"Miles, did you have to do it that way?"

He stiffened suddenly at the change in her tone. "Do what?"

"Stage the whole thing as a kind of challenge to Page Wilburn? At first I thought — well, I thought you were attracted to her. But tonight I realized you only wanted to make clear to her that she had better not push Norman Graham around. The way he glared at her! It was really embarrassing, and I felt sorry for the poor girl."

Forrest shrugged. "You let little things bother you. And you are tired because the party dragged out so long."

"Actually it didn't. It just seemed long. Wasn't it bad luck about the lights on the terrace! I've never known that to happen before."

He looked at her quickly, looked away. "You seemed so upset when you came in with the Wilburn girl I wondered what was wrong."

"I don't know. She was almost in a state of shock. Her hands were like ice. Maybe she's one of those silly women who are terrified of the dark. I don't know —" Ruth Forrest's voice trailed off.

Almost furtively, the eyes of husband and wife met in the mirror.

"Ruth," he said gently, "tell me the truth. Why did you go out there in the dark, looking for Miss Wilburn?"

"Let's not talk any more," she said sharply. "I'm tired and I have a headache. I'm going to bed."

SIXTEEN

VANCE COOPER pulled out a chair across from the head of the security division, took the jade pendant from his pocket and pushed it across the desk.

"From now on this is your baby," he said. "I'm taking no more chances on Miss Wilburn's safety."

The security man was ruffled by Vance's undisguised anger. "We have two people guarding her at all times," he said stiffly.

"Not closely enough. Not carefully enough. Last night, at Miles Forrest's dinner party, someone tried to throw her off the parapet. It's a twenty-story drop from that penthouse."

For an appalled moment the security man stared at him. "My God!" he breathed. He reached for his telephone, dialed, tapped a pencil impatiently while the phone rang and rang.

At length a girl's voice said sleepily, "Hello?"

"Jane?"

"Yes, sir," she said, wide awake now that she recognized her boss's voice.

"Didn't you get a job at the Forrest apartment last night for the dinner party?"

"Yes, sir."

"Anything to report?"

"I was going to call in later. I think Miss Wilburn recognized me. She saw me once before at a hotel. I thought it was probably just as well to let her know I was your operative. Make her feel more secure. I sort of smiled and nodded at her."

"Well?"

"I managed to slip a note into her jacket pocket, suggesting that Marta Wentley has some association with Jerome Brooks. I was following Miss Wilburn when she went down to the Wentley girl's place in the Village yesterday. After she left there your other operative picked her up. So I hung around for a few minutes and I was just leaving when Brooks came out. I couldn't figure whether the Wilburn girl had seen him or not, but I got the impression she didn't know about him. Something about the way he looked around, not wanting to be noticed. So I thought she ought to be warned."

"In the future, leave policy decisions to me. Is that clear?"

"Yes, sir," she said, abashed. "But why you have to call me now I can't understand. I've been on duty twelve hours a day."

"Last night while you were at the Forrest apartment someone tried to throw Miss Wilburn off the terrace."

"Oh, no!" It was a cry of horror. "That must have been when the lights went out. How awful. But, after all, what could I have done? I wasn't expected to mingle with the guests. I had to stay down on the lower floor."

"I suppose you did the best you could. Do you know anything about that light failure?"

"I heard one of the servants say that someone must have blown a fuse. There was nothing really wrong at all. Honestly I can't see —"

"I suppose you did the best you could, Jane," he said grudgingly. "All right, go back to sleep."

He slammed down the telephone and glowered at Vance. "Well, that's the way the breaks go sometimes. You can't watch everything all the time." He picked up the jade figurine, turned it curiously in his hand. "Any nibbles?"

"That wasn't the reason for last night's attack," Vance said. "Page Wilburn wasn't wearing it when she was nearly thrown off the terrace."

"Then why was she attacked? You know, Mr. Cooper, that girl may be as beautiful as they say, but she certainly has an exceptional talent for making enemies. When I saw Graham yesterday — and I must admit he came voluntarily, bringing that receipt for the mink jacket — he was in a mood to wring her pretty neck. He believes she planted it on him."

"Why?" Vance asked.

"Needed a fall guy, apparently."

"Someone," Vance said softly, "certainly needs a fall guy."

At his tone the other man's eyes narrowed. "Do you have any ideas?"

"Ideas, yes. Evidence, no."

"Go ahead. Give. We could use some ideas around here."

"You won't like mine," Vance said.

He was quite right. When he had finished talking the security man shook his head, kept on shaking it. "No — and no — and no. That's about the wildest —" He paused, swiveled his chair so that he stared out of the window, then swiveled back to face Vance.

After thinking for a while he said, "To get back to Miss Wilburn's capacity for making enemies, it doesn't seem to be confined to Markham employees or even people concerned with Operation Homebase. We are using almost as many operatives as we have engineers. One of them was helping to string wires and put in bulbs for lighting the terrace at the Forrest place. This was before the party, of course. He heard Mrs. Forrest going at it hot and heavy. She kept hammering at Forrest and hammering at him. Apparently she is jealous and suspicious. My operative said no girl who had ever played around with Forrest had better meet his wife on a dark night." He broke off. "Oh, ridiculous!" He dismissed his own thought with an impatient gesture.

"Anyhow," Vance pointed out, "Mrs. Forrest did not attack Miss Wilburn. She probably saved her life. What I can't figure out is how it could have happened."

"I suppose it was just a question of watching for an opportunity. *If* she came around the side of the terrace, *if* she happened to be alone — it wouldn't take more than seconds to throw the switch, seconds more to reach her — and seconds in which to disappear when Mrs. Forrest so opportunely arrived."

The two men considered the matter. "I imagine," Vance said, "there is another door from the terrace to the apartment. You might check with your operatives. In that way some person — if you don't like my identification —"

"I don't."

"— could slip back to the party without being noticed."

"Personally, I am inclined to put my money on Graham," the security head said. "A guy who goes around offering diamond necklaces —"

"I can explain that," Vance told him. And he did. There was no indication whether he was believed or not.

When Vance had reported the presence of the ferret-faced man in the elevator, the other man made a gesture of despair. "That fellow is like a gas leak. Evidence of him everywhere and yet we can't track him down. Who is he working for? That's what I want to know. Whoever he is, he is always just a step ahead of us."

"Are you keeping an eye on Kate Willing, the girl who is masquerading as my aunt's goddaughter, Beverly Main?"

"She is living at the Beekman Tower under the name of Main. She still goes back and forth to her apartment on Washington Square, which she retains under the name of Willing. Down there she meets a good-looking young fellow, according to the man we have following her."

"Does he seem to be the one who is paying the rent and buying mink jackets?"

"I wouldn't say so. We haven't enough men to follow everyone, Cooper. As it is we are keeping a dozen people working full time, trying to check on the people chiefly involved. What we can't do is to link them up."

"For my money, you don't know a link when you see one," Vance said emphatically.

Again the security man said a stubborn, "No." Then he added, "Make some other links, if you can." There was a challenge in his voice.

"There's a link from the mink jacket Kate Willing is wearing to Norman Graham who had a receipt for the jacket."

"Which he says was planted on him. And, remember, we failed to get an identification of him at the fur store."

"I agree that the receipt was planted on him," Vance said quietly. "Nothing will convince me that Graham isn't meant to be a fall guy."

"Any more links?"

Vance's face set. "Yes," he said levelly, "there is an apparent link between my cousin Marta Wentley and that jade pendant. Someone is priming Marta about what goes on in the house she hasn't entered for five years. And someone primed Kate Willing about the family so she could step into the shoes of Beverly Main."

"You think they have provided each other with the information?"

"I'm terribly afraid so. On my aunt's account as much as on Marta's I wish I didn't believe it. But I can't see any alternative. Marta is obstinate, but she isn't a strong character. She is easily led, easily influenced. I don't believe she has any idea what she is involved in. But she still resents her mother's former dominance and I think it is possible she thought it would be a joke to plant a stranger in the house who would take in her mother completely and make her see she isn't infallible."

"And how do you establish the link between Kate Willing and your cousin Marta?"

"I'd be guessing."

"You've done a lot of guessing," the security head said dryly.

"I suspect, as your operative suggested, it may be Jerome Brooks."

An amused smile played around the other man's mouth. "I must admit you have a lot of ideas."

"And there isn't one of them I like," Vance said as he got to his feet. "I was wondering —"

"What now?"

"Is Operation Homebase worth it?" He turned on his heel and went out of the room, leaving the other man to stare after him.

ii

That was not the only question being asked that day. In the small tool shed off the terrace of her penthouse, Mrs. Forrest studied the fuse box. She picked up the fuse that lay on the floor, pushed it in, and lights gleamed palely against the daylight in loops and festoons around the terrace.

After a quick look around, she came out of the shed, strolled quietly back into the living room, went downstairs to adjust a small black hat, pull a sable cape over her trim gray suit, draw on long white gloves. At her nod the doorman whistled for a taxi.

The driver, turning to slam the door which she had left unlatched, saw her face. A pretty woman, he thought, but she seemed to be mighty worried about something. Wearing that kind of fur, living in that kind of building, and she thought she had worries! He could tell her about worries.

At least it was a nice long haul, he thought in satisfaction. All the way down to Wall Street. There the woman's graceful figure was scooped off the street by revolving doors, moved along a corridor, paused for a moment to check a name against the huge directory of tenants, rose swiftly to the fortieth floor. BAINES & MISTON, *Brokers,* read the sign on the door.

It was Mr. Baines whom Ruth Forrest wanted to see. Mr. Baines, though a busy and important man, saw her promptly, coming into the reception room to greet her and leading her back to his big corner office where she could get a breathtaking view of the Statue of Liberty.

Ruth Forrest asked her question.

"Yes," Mr. Baines assured her. "It is all in your name."

iii

The woman's voice was young and pleasant. "Norman? This is Leslie Trevor."

"Well, what are you doing in New York?"

"A shopping spree. How about taking a girl to lunch?"

"Delighted."

"The Gotham at one?" she suggested.

"Can you make it twelve-thirty?"

"Of course."

At twelve-thirty, Norman Graham, followed unobtrusively by the operative who had been assigned to him, strolled into the Gotham. The young engineer checked his hat and overcoat, looked around the lobby, and settled down to wait. Then a girl came up to him, a good-looking girl, the operative thought in approval.

"Norman Graham?" she asked.

He stood up, nodding.

"Leslie is terribly sorry. She had a fitting and couldn't make it. She sent me along to pinch hit." The girl laughed. "That sounds as though I were forcing myself on you for lunch, doesn't it?"

As it obviously did, there was nothing Graham could say.

"Actually my only excuse for being here is that I've got a lot of messages for you from — uh — San Francisco."

"Come on." Norman's face lighted up. He took her arm, nodded to the headwaiter who found them a table for two.

Later the operative reported, "I couldn't get close enough to hear anything they said. All I'm sure of is that Graham lied when he said he didn't know Kate Willing. He was lunching with her and he seemed to like it."

iv

Another lunch table was sloppily set, the canned soup was only tepid and the sandwiches were unappetizing. The girl and the young man faced each other across the table.

"Sweet Thing," he said cajolingly, "nothing has changed between us. Nothing ever will."

"You were angry with me," she whimpered. "Terribly angry with me. I did it for you. All the time I've done it for you. And then you were angry with me."

He smiled at her. He had a very attractive smile. "You were saying things you shouldn't say."

"Well, that Wilburn girl said I wasn't attractive, and she criticized the way I live, and she thinks my mother is right about everything, and she — and she — "

"So you let her know you'd been told about her and about what goes on in your mother's house."

"Well —" She saw his expression. There was a pleading tone in her voice. "You aren't mad at me still? Say you aren't mad at me."

He did not relent. She was as pliable as a piece of string, he thought. As easy to manage. As easy to cut off when one had enough. She capitulated, as he had known she would.

"What do you want me to do now?" she asked him.

He told her.

v

The connection was poor and Page had difficulty in hearing what the distraught girl at the other end of the line was saying.

"Helen!" she exclaimed at last. "Where are you? . . .
San Francisco? . . . What in the world —"

"Norman just called me," Helen said. "He is almost
out of his mind. He told me about what you have been doing and it doesn't sound like you at all. The very last person
to act like that!"

"But what did he say?" Page was puzzled.

"He said he believed you the day you lunched with him.
He believed you weren't trying to get him into trouble at
Markham's. And then —" She went on with an incoherent
account of the security check-up and the planting of the receipt for the mink jacket in Norman's apartment. "And then
today a girl called him, pretending to be Leslie Trevor and
asked him to take her to lunch. And who would know about
Leslie except you?"

"But, Helen —"

"And it wasn't Leslie at all. It was a girl he'd never seen
before. At first she pretended she had messages from me.
And then, when she made a slip and he knew it wasn't true,
she just sat smiling at him. She'd tricked him into lunching
with her so the Markham people would think — and I believe him," Helen concluded. "No matter what anyone says.
He's been a perfect dope, of course, to try to be like my father. But he isn't dishonest. He couldn't be, Page! And he
thinks you —"

Page broke in to tell her side of the story.

"Well," Helen said on a long breath, "you are certainly
mixed up in something strange. Who could possibly be trying to injure Norman? Who could have tried to throw you
off that terrace?"

SEVENTEEN

"MISS MAIN to see you," Perkins said.

Mrs. Wentley looked up from the small desk where she was busy making lists of guests for the party she must give for Vance and Page. She had been working with a heavy heart, wishing that she could trust the girl whom Vance seemed to love so deeply, the girl who appeared on the surface to be honest, loyal, utterly trustworthy. She must, she supposed, include her goddaughter among the guests, but it would be awkward for more than one reason. Beverly not only was in love with Vance but she distrusted Page and she was, understandably, jealous of her.

"Send her up, and will you serve tea in about a quarter of an hour?"

The girl ran up the stairs. Last time Mrs. Wentley had seen her she had been dejected, uncertain whether to stay in the city now that Vance was engaged to another girl. Today she seemed to have recovered her good spirits.

"Dear Mrs. Wentley!" she exclaimed.

"Sit down, Beverly. How are you getting along?"

The girl looked from the cluttered desk to Mrs. Wentley's face. "I hope I'm not interrupting anything important."

"No, I was just drawing up some plans for a small reception for Page. I'm afraid most of my friends are rather elderly for her but they've known Vance all his life and they would expect to be included in a party that announced his engagement. Of course, if Marta —" The words were cut off. "If you won't find it too boring, I'll send you a card."

"How kind of you." Unexpectedly Beverly came to put her arm around the older woman, to kiss her cheek. "But you are always kind. Somehow, I feel at times as though you were my own mother."

Mrs. Wentley's withdrawal was so slight it was hardly discernible. She did not return the caress. "I am afraid," she said, "there is no substitute for a real mother — or a real daughter."

Her tired but observant eyes saw the subtle alteration in her goddaughter's expression, the compression of her lips, a flash of anger almost instantly controlled.

"So really," Beverly said, as though she had not been aware of Mrs. Wentley's withdrawal or her reproof, "you are going to be the one to announce the engagement. I assume from that the girl has no family of her own."

"No, she lost her mother several years ago and her father within the past year."

"Actually, then," and Beverly's eyes were very sharp, "no one knows much about her. She might have come out of nowhere."

Mrs. Wentley made no reply and the silence between the two women dragged on, became rather awkward for the visitor. Her hostess remained relaxed, withdrawn, dignified.

"You are putting a brave face on it," Beverly said at last, "but I know how devoted you are to Vance. How much you want his happiness. Mrs. Wentley, I implore you not to involve yourself any further in this — this distasteful engagement. I can't appeal to Vance. He wouldn't believe a word I say."

"Would you expect him to be disloyal to the girl he wants to make his wife?"

"I think the facts have to be faced, Mrs. Wentley. I am positive that Page Wilburn is wearing a piece of stolen jewelry." As Mrs. Wentley started to protest she held up her hand. "We could settle it once and for all if I could check that jade pendant against the one that was advertised. Do you think that is unfair? After all, I love him too. If I am wrong, then I will withdraw, knowing that all is well with him. Otherwise —"

"Otherwise?" Mrs. Wentley asked.

"I won't give him up, not without a fight, and a fight in the open. It's my belief that Page Wilburn is a thief and a liar."

"Beverly!"

"I had friends of mine in San Francisco look her up. Her reputation is bad, Mrs. Wentley. The number of men she plays around with — well, Vance might not mind, but at least he should have his eyes opened."

"And you intend to open his eyes."

"All I want is to know for sure about that jade figurine. Is it or is it not the one described in the advertisement? Is that so unreasonable?"

Mrs. Wentley looked down at the neat list of names, at the address book, at her pen. She was trying desperately to balance Page's deep, honest eyes against this girl's accusations; to balance Vance's love for Page against the strange searching of her room; to balance what seemed to be Page's radiant happiness in Vance's love against her stormy interview with the handsome young man who had brought her roses and her lunch engagement with another man whom she had not identified.

With a little gesture of defeat she got to her feet, walked to the bookshelves, pulled down the old leather-bound book which had been turned into a box. Opened it.

It was empty.

"This is where she has been keeping the pendant," she said blankly. "Vance calls it Page's private safe. I can't understand what she can have done with it, what has happened. She wasn't wearing it when she went out to-day."

Perkins came up with the tea tray and Mrs. Wentley seated herself behind it. "Sugar?" she asked. "Lemon or cream?" She asked more sharply, "Are you all right?"

"A little dizzy. No tea, thank you, Mrs. Wentley. I must be going."

The girl who called herself Beverly Main went down the circular staircase so swiftly that Perkins was barely able to reach the door in time to open it for her.

Mrs. Wentley, leaving the tea tray untouched, returned to her desk, picked up the unfinished list and, with an abrupt gesture, tore the sheet of paper into small bits and dropped them in a wastebasket.

ii

By the time she had dressed for dinner, Vance had changed and was waiting in the sitting room. He stood leaning on the mantel, staring down into the empty grate. How distinguished he was, his aunt thought proudly. There was a new sternness in his face, and she watched him for a moment in concern.

Then Page's door opened and she came out. Vance's face lighted up. He held out his arms and Page walked into them. Seeing her expression Mrs. Wentley thought: She can't be dishonest. She loves him as deeply as he loves her. Then what is wrong?

Over Page's shoulder Vance saw his aunt, kissed Page and released her.

"For once I am home early," he said, "with time to talk to my two girls."

"I'm glad," Mrs. Wentley said, though she did not sound glad. "I wanted — that is, I feel that I must talk to you both."

"What's wrong, Aunt Jane?" Vance seemed to brace tired shoulders, prepared for some new problem.

She sat facing them, her eyes on her long slim hands in which veins were beginning to show. "This afternoon Beverly Main came to see me. She had — certain allegations to make. This isn't the first time she has done so but I felt — it seems to me that we'll have to discuss this thing quite frankly."

Vance's eyes narrowed in speculation but he did not seem concerned. He smiled at Page who was sitting beside him on the couch, reached for her hand, held it clasped in his.

"Beverly," Mrs. Wentley seemed to have trouble in expressing herself, "made certain statements about Page. She — well, she more or less claims that Page — stole that piece of jade she has been wearing. She demanded to see it. I — I wanted to reassure her." Mrs. Wentley sent an unhappy look at Page. "For your sake, my dear. For Vance's. So I looked in that old book Vance calls your private safe. The pendant wasn't there." Again she paused unhappily. She looked up to find Vance smiling broadly.

"And then what did Beverly do?" he asked.

"She wasn't feeling well. She left abruptly. She didn't even wait for tea, though I was just starting to pour it. I've wondered since if I should have let her go when she was feeling dizzy."

Vance laughed. "Anything else?"

"She — Beverly — had some rather unpleasant things to say about Page." After a moment Mrs. Wentley went on, a break in her voice, "I'm so terribly sorry, Vance."

He laughed again. "Well, I suppose I should have taken you into my confidence in the beginning." He didn't, to her astonishment, seem at all upset.

"Vance," Page warned him, "please don't. Not yet. Not until we are sure."

"It's all right," he told her. "You see, Aunt Jane, I hate deceiving you about anything but you — you aren't very good at hiding your real feelings, are you?"

"What on earth do you mean?"

"I mean that when you dislike or distrust anyone, or even when you feel critical, you — let it show. What I am going to tell you now is very important. Whatever your feelings are, you must not reveal them to anyone. Is that clear?"

As he had never in his life spoken to her like that she stared at him in astonishment. "There is nothing clear about it. What on earth is this all about? So far as I can see, you don't put much weight on what my goddaughter has to say."

"Actually," Vance told her coolly, "I haven't the faintest idea what your goddaughter would have to say about anything. How could I? I've never laid eyes on the girl in my life."

"Oh, Vance," Page protested, "you needn't sound so

mysterious. You're just bewildering Aunt Jane and it's bad enough without that." She too seemed to be undisturbed by Beverly's accusations.

"About three months ago," Vance said, "your god-daughter, Beverly Main, whom you hadn't seen since she was five, suddenly began to appear on the scene. She got herself invited here as a weekend guest; she came to the house whenever she could. That was her idea but, I suspect, somewhere along the line, the suggestion might have been planted that she might be a nice wife for Vance."

Mrs. Wentley made a deprecating gesture, but there was a faint flush on her cheeks.

"So, because I was involved in a very hush-hush job at Markham's and anything unusual had to be checked, I had Beverly Main checked as a security measure."

"Really, Vance!" Mrs. Wentley was angry. "That is go-ing too far: my own house, my guest, my goddaughter."

"Your house and your guest," he agreed, "but not your goddaughter. Beverly Main got married and moved to Australia four years ago. She has never come back to this country."

"But —"

"The girl who is trying to pass herself off as your god-daughter is Kate Willing. At least that is the name under which she has had an apartment on Washington Square for the past three months."

"You must be wrong, Vance. You simply must be wrong. Beverly knows all about you and me; all about our back-ground. All about her parents' background. She even knows about — Marta, though I suppose you told her that. She expected to have Marta's room, you know."

"I have never mentioned Marta to her, but she has been very well briefed indeed, Aunt Jane." Mrs. Wentley heard the pity in her nephew's voice. "Very well briefed. She even has a key to this house. Where do you think she got that key?"

"Vance!" Page was imploring him to stop, but he shook his head.

"It's kinder to face the whole truth," he said.

His aunt was watching him carefully now, her hands gripped hard together. After a moment she asked, her voice hoarse, "Why would someone try to pretend to be Beverly? What was there to gain by it?"

"I suppose that depends on the person. So far as Kate herself is concerned there were several reasons. First, she wanted an inside track to me not only because I'm second man at Markham's but because, being a gal on the make if there ever was one, she thought she might profit by the fact that Marta had gone, that there might be pickings for her. And as I wasn't married I might support her as well as the next man. But what she wanted most, what she wants desperately, is that jade figurine."

Mrs. Wentley put a shaking hand to her temple. "I am so bewildered —"

"I'll have to start at the beginning," Vance said, and did so. He began with the awareness that there was a leak of valuable information, with Markham's star agent discovering the method by which secret information was being taken abroad, with Page stumbling by accident on what apparently was the password and getting the jade figurine.

"It was a bad break all around," Vance explained. "You see, by this time we had already involved Page; that is,

Markham and I had involved her. The idea was to keep Beverly — or whoever she might turn out to be, we hadn't established her identity then — out of this house. So Page was brought in to pose as my fiancée."

"To pose —"

Vance's smile was broader, brighter. "It's all right, Aunt Jane. That part is all right. Page and I have found that we belong together."

"Thank heaven that one thing is clear," Mrs. Wentley said. She looked from face to face. "And right. I'm so happy for you both."

"A lot of things are clear now," Vance told her, and again there was pity in his voice. He explained about Page's wearing the jade figurine and the dangers in which it had involved her. "Right now the security branch has the jade, and Page won't ever have to wear it again. But she can't really be safe until we have cleared up the whole mess."

Something in his voice made Page exclaim, "You think you know who it is!"

"I think so, but I must admit that I can't get anyone to agree with me."

"I do."

"You know? How?"

"I don't know. Only that hand over my mouth last night — my lip was cut again — I —"

"There is bound to be evidence somewhere," he said, "to prove we are right."

"I hope you find it before Norman Graham is completely discredited." Page told him about her long-distance call from Helen. "I suppose that was Kate Willing, snaring Norman into going to lunch with her, making sure the connection was plain, setting him up as the traitor."

"Look here, Page, my darling, you didn't tell her who you thought was behind this."

"Yes, I did. She thought I was doing that horrible thing to Norman. What else could I have done, Vance?"

"You know what will happen — has probably happened already?" She had never seen him so upset. She shook her head. "Your friend Helen probably didn't waste a minute in calling Norman back to say that you are in the clear, that you believe —"

"Oh!"

"For God's sake, be careful, Page. If you were in danger before you are in more danger now."

After looking at her nephew's strained face, Mrs. Wentley said, "I don't understand why Page should be in danger here, Vance."

"Have you had the locks changed yet?"

"Why no."

"But you realize, don't you, that someone has a key to this house?"

Into the pool of silence came Mrs. Wentley's little sigh. "Oh, that's it, isn't it, Vance? You think Marta is involved in this ugliness, in this treachery. You think it was her key — you think she told Beverly, or whoever this girl may be, about us." She put her hands over her face. "What have I done to my child, Vance? What have I made of her?"

He came to perch on the arm of her chair, to draw her hands gently away from her face, holding them in his.

"One of the world's favorite pastimes seems to be blaming parents for what their children turn out to be. I think it is stupid and dishonest to blame someone else for the kind of person we become. In the long run I think people are made by the choices they make. I think they end by doing what they want to do. I don't say, doing what makes them happiest. That's something quite different. For the most part, people choose their own unhappiness too."

"But to think of Marta's being a traitor. I can't bear it."

"No, Aunt Jane!" Page protested. "I don't believe that for a single minute. I don't think she has the slightest idea what she is involved in."

"How would you know?" Mrs. Wentley asked. "You don't know Marta."

"I've seen her." Page described her talk with Marta. She tried to mitigate nothing, but she did stress the girl's essential loneliness, her forlorn quality.

"I think she knows she was wrong in leaving you the way she did, but she doesn't know how to change things. She hasn't the — the grace to come back and tell you she was wrong. And, anyhow, I imagine she is afraid you wouldn't forgive her."

"Forgive her? I could forgive her any — that is, you're sure she isn't involved in betraying her country?"

"Not knowingly," Page was firm about that. "What I think is that she is being used by someone who knows her background, used to provide Kate Willing with information on Beverly and on you and Vance. I imagine Marta thought she was playing a kind of practical joke on you, letting some phony come into your house and fool you, to prove to you that your judgment could be wrong. The — the other part — no, I don't think she has any idea. I tried to warn her."

"You went to see Marta because you suspected that she was involved in all this?"

Page shook her head. "No, Aunt Jane, I went because

you wanted her. I thought perhaps I could talk her into coming back."

"And you couldn't." It was not a question.

"There is someone who seems to have a great deal of influence over her. But in the long run — in the long run, Aunt Jane, I believe Marta will refuse to do anything really wrong."

Mrs. Wentley got up, kissed Page's cheek. "Bless you, my dear," she said huskily. "I am more grateful to you than I can say. Vance, I am so glad that you have found Page."

"So am I," he told her.

Perkins came quietly up the circular staircase to announce that dinner was served.

When he had gone she looked from one to the other. "What can I do?" she asked. "You are both doing so much, risking so much."

"There is nothing you can do but wait," Vance told her. "But, Aunt Jane, if your so-called goddaughter should telephone or come here —"

"I won't admit her, of course."

"No, no! You must see her. And there must be no difference in your manner. A lot depends on you. Can you do that? Can you be sure that no shadow of suspicion appears in your face, no distrust in your voice, no hostility in your manner?"

"I can do that," she promised, and led the way down the stairs to the dining room.

EIGHTEEN

"SO IT'S you again." Marta waited while Page climbed the second long flight of stairs. "What do you want this time?"

"I'd like to talk to you, if I may."

"Go ahead if you think it will do any good." Marta leaned against a chair, looking mockingly at Page. As usual she wore tight blue jeans, a tight sweater, her hair hung lank and straight around her face. As usual, too, she failed in her attempt to look tough. She looked like a neglected child, much younger than her years, perhaps because she had never matured. Even at twenty-three she was still a spoiled schoolgirl.

Today, as Page saw in the first glance, the curtain of the little closet was open. Aside from a few untidy garments there was nothing inside. Nobody inside.

"Do sit down," Marta said, again in that mocking tone. "Or do you prefer to deliver your sermons standing?"

"I'm not going to preach to you," Page said. "I'm not even going to beg you to return home as I did the last time, though you could give your mother more happiness than you could easily imagine if you were to go. And you'd be — freer than you are now."

"What do you mean by that?" Marta's tone was shrill.

"I mean you think you have escaped from your mother's domination, but you have only submitted to a worse domination, something ugly, something terrible."

Marta laughed softly. "You wouldn't be jealous, would you?"

And then Page knew that the operative who had put the note in her pocket was right.

"No, Marta, I'm not jealous. Not of Jerry."

"I didn't say —"

"Look, you are going to hate this; you are going to try not to believe me. I can understand that. Once I was in love with Jerry too. Before I knew what he was like."

"You mean before he jilted you."

"Yes," Page said steadily, "before he jilted me. He broke our engagement because I didn't have enough money to keep him in the style to which he wanted to become accustomed. There's a name for men like that, Marta. It isn't a nice name."

"Jealous," Marta repeated. "I don't want to hear anything about Jerry."

"Poor Marta," Page said gently.

Marta's face flamed with anger. "And I don't need your pity."

"Jerry is using you," Page said. "He needs you as a tool to serve his own ends."

"He loves me!"

"I tried to warn you before, but he was here then, wasn't he, Marta? Hiding behind that curtain. Rather a cowardly thing to do, wasn't it, while he told you what to say."

Marta's lips parted, closed again. "You're just trying to get even with Jerry. There is no way he could use me. That's silly. Just tell me how he could."

"I can tell you that. He wanted to get Kate Willing into your mother's house, posing as Beverly Main. He used you to provide Kate with the background material that would make it possible for her to fool your mother. You thought it would be fun, didn't you, to make a fool of your mother? A kind of childish joke, like pulling out a chair from behind someone."

"Well, she —"

"Why do you think Jerry would go to so much trouble to help you play a practical joke on your mother? He wanted Kate there to spy on Vance because he is involved in a hush-hush job. And later he wanted her to get hold of that jade figurine I was wearing."

Page saw the sudden change in Marta's expression.

"Do you know why he is so eager to get hold of that piece of jade, Marta?"

"I — I don't want to hear. I won't listen." Marta covered her ears like a child refusing to face the truth.

"Yes, you are going to listen. You were being used to help betray your country."

"Not Jerry," Marta said, "not Jerry. Jerry loves me."

"I'll bet that's what Kate Willing thinks too," Page told her. "It's what he said to me only a few days ago. Nothing was changed between us. He wanted to renew our engagement. Jerry believes every girl will fall for him, and I guess most of them do. I did myself. Once."

"No!"

"But you told Kate about your mother and Vance and about Beverly's background, didn't you? And you did it because Jerry told you to."

Page held Marta's eyes, her suggestible eyes. They wavered. "Yes," she said at last.

"And it was Jerry who brought Kate to you, Jerry who

suggested this practical joke you could play on your mother."

"Yes — well, I don't remember — and it's not the way you think —"

"How did you meet him?"

"Oh, I was sitting on a bench in Washington Square and he came along. We got to talking. No matter what you say, he liked me a lot. Right from the first. He understood me. So I told him who I really was —"

"Do you think he didn't know that? Don't you know you were set up for just one reason, to get Kate into your mother's house?"

"No!"

Page sighed and turned to go. "I've done my best," she said. "Not only for Aunt Jane and Vance but for you too. I've told you the truth, Marta. I know it's hard to believe, that you don't want to believe Jerry hasn't been honest about loving you, that he is involving you in great trouble, in dishonor. But even if you don't believe me, don't let yourself be used any more. For your own sake. For the sake of your country."

"Is that all you have to say?" Marta sounded hard, but her eyes were frightened.

"That's all."

Page went out of the room and she did not look back. She walked slowly down the stairs, wondering what more she could have done, what more she could have said. In all honesty she had to admit that if anyone had told her Jerry's love was not real she would have refused to believe until he himself had made it all too clear.

She strolled along Fourth Street, then aimlessly for a few

blocks, stopping to look in the window of a book and print shop. At last she turned back, wondering whether it would be worthwhile returning to Marta's to make one last appeal. Then she saw Marta cross Washington Square, enter a big apartment building. This was the building from which she had seen the man she had believed to be Jerry emerging.

Almost running, Page entered the building in time to hear Marta say, "Miss Willing, please." The operator pushed in plugs, lights flashed on the board. "Miss Mary Smith to see you," he said and nodded to Marta, who went swiftly to the elevator. She did not notice Page.

ii

"Miss Marta!" Perkins flung open the door of the little house on Murray Hill.

"Hello, Perkins." Marta came in slowly, turning for a swift look along the street behind her before the door closed.

"Mrs. Wentley is — is — upstairs," Perkins said, almost stuttering in surprise.

There was a sardonic smile around Marta's mouth. She's lost her looks, the houseman thought with regret. She sure has lost her looks. And those clothes! Mrs. Wentley will have a fit.

"I can find my way, Perkins," Marta said, and went swiftly across the drawing room, more slowly up the stairs. Before reaching the top she stopped, gripping the railing for a moment.

There was a cry. "Marta!"

Perkins waited, but there was no further sound. He went softly back to his own quarters where he told his wife about it in whispers, though there was no danger of being overheard.

"So she's back!" Mrs. Perkins said in satisfaction. "And high time. The way her mother has just been pining away. But keeping a good face on it. Never a word. I guess she's about the happiest woman in the world right now."

"Well," Perkins said, considering, "I wouldn't know about that."

"I tell you she just worshiped that girl. Next to her husband, of course."

"You haven't seen her yet," Perkins said.

"What's wrong?"

"She's changed a lot. And it's not just her clothes. Regular beatnik she is now. But her ways are different too. I don't know why she's come back, but there is something wrong about her expression. I don't think she cares a rap about her mother's feelings. She's up to something, you mark my words," Perkins said darkly.

"Where's she going to stay, that's what I'd like to know, with Miss Wilburn in her room?"

"If I know Miss Marta she'll have Miss Wilburn out before she knows it. Or maybe she could move into Mr. Cooper's room. Someone else will have to move. Miss Marta is not one to put herself out for someone else. She never was."

"At least," his wife said, "she's home. I don't care why. Her mother must have been worried sick. How could she help it? The girl was only eighteen when she left home, and young for her age."

There was no doubt about Mrs. Wentley's feelings. She held out her arms and Marta, after standing at the top of the stairs, one hand in a pocket of her jeans, came slowly forward.

Mrs. Wentley's arms dropped to her sides. "Marta," she

said softly. "Marta." As though it was enough just to speak her daughter's name.

The big, tired-looking eyes watched her warily, found nothing but love and welcome in her mother's face, and then the pain that followed her lack of response.

She held out her hand, almost shyly, and took her mother's. For some reason she found it difficult to meet her mother's eyes.

She cleared her throat. "I've come back," she said a trifle defiantly, a trifle dubiously, "if that's all right."

"All right!" Again there was that undisguised joy in her mother's voice. But there was no word of criticism, nothing to remind Marta of the pain and anxiety she had caused, no question as to where she had been or what she had done, no comment on the way she was dressed. Nothing but welcome and love and joy.

"Well, I didn't know how you would feel."

"Just having you back, just having you back. There's nothing else in the world I could wish for."

Marta looked around. "Nothing seems to have changed here. And you still have faithful old Perkins."

"No," her mother answered, "nothing much changes here." But everything had changed, of course. A beloved daughter had rejected her, had disappeared, had remained away for five long and painful years. Now she had reappeared but, instinct told Mrs. Wentley, something was wrong. She remembered Page saying that someone was influencing Marta. She had a curious feeling that Marta had returned not because she wanted to, not out of affection or concern for her mother. She was obeying a stronger will than her own.

But she was Marta, she was her daughter, she was home

and safe. In spite of herself her hand tightened on Marta's, her eyes filled with tears.

Marta looked at her almost in surprise. It was as though, concerned only with herself, she had never before really been aware of her mother except as a stumbling block to her own undisciplined wishes. And without warning she was on her knees beside her mother's chair, her head on her mother's breast, her mother's arms around her, the sobs ripping through her, shaking her thin body.

Her mother rocked her as though she were a baby, saying gently, "There, there," letting the storm exhaust itself.

A long time later Marta drew away, got to her feet, wiping off her tears childishly with her hand.

"I'm sorry," she said, but she did not explain. Again her mother asked no questions. "As long as you are here," she said, and Marta's mouth grimaced as though with pain.

"I shouldn't have done it," Marta tried once more.

"You mean you shouldn't have sent Kate Willing here."

Marta's eyes widened. "How did you know?"

"Vance knows. Page knows."

"Well, I only did it as a joke. I mean —"

"You thought the girl could deceive me," Mrs. Wentley said. "Well, of course she did. But when she tried to take your place — I could not have that. No one else could ever do that."

She was looking down at her hands now, as though she feared to see Marta's revealing face.

"I guess it was pretty mean of me," Marta said inadequately.

"But there is one thing, Marta," and now Mrs. Wentley's voice changed. "There is something more important than you and I are. You must not let Kate Willing know that I have been told who she really is. Vance has warned me. It might cause great trouble. You will be very careful, won't you?"

Marta's eyes widened. She brushed her hair away from her face, turned away from her mother's eyes. "Why, sure," she said unconvincingly. "Why, of course. I won't say anything." She added hastily, "I'd like to have a bath in a real tub for a change. There's only a shower at that lousy room where I've been living."

"Page is out so you can use your own room. And your clothes — that is, the ones I got you — are hanging in the big closet off my room."

"I — thanks." Marta turned away hastily, as though escaping from the scrutiny that made her so uneasy. "I'll make an appointment with Elizabeth Arden. I need my hair cut. Perhaps they can fit me in this afternoon. And I'll move out Page's stuff. I want my own room. Naturally."

She hastened away, a girl in flight, and her mother looked after her, eyes somber. What have I done to her, she wondered bleakly. What have I made of my daughter? She is lying to me. I don't know why she has come back, but there is a wrong reason.

iii

When Page came in from an afternoon's shopping she found Mrs. Wentley waiting for her.

"Marta has come back. Right now she is at Elizabeth Arden's, but she has come home to stay. She — of course, she wanted her own room, so she put your things in Vance's room. He can go to his club."

"As long as she is here, I'm not really needed in

the house," Page told her. "After all, the idea was simply to keep out Kate Willing. So I can go to a hotel."

"Let's wait and find out what Vance wants," Mrs. Wentley suggested.

Page saw that the older woman was deeply distressed. Her daughter's homecoming had not brought the pleasure, the relief, it had been intended to. In Vance's room Page looked at her clothes, dresses, underwear, shoes, everything tumbled together and tossed on the floor. For a moment she was shaken with rage. Then she picked them up, hung dresses in Vance's closet. There was a childish vindictiveness in Marta's action that puzzled her. Was she behaving in this malicious way because she was bitter with Page for telling her the truth about Jerry, or was she deliberately attempting to drive her out of the Murray Hill house? And, if that was the idea, had Marta received her orders when she had gone to Kate's apartment?

Page changed hastily so that Vance's room would be free for him when he came home. Tonight she put on the soft rose-pink dress that matched the jade engagement ring. She hoped that she would have an opportunity to talk to Vance before Marta came home.

But when she came out of Vance's room she learned that Marta had already come home and was in her room dressing for dinner. Unfortunately Marta had finished before Vance returned. When she appeared, her hair cut short and waved closely to her head like a sleek cap, wearing an evening dress of old-gold velvet, Page looked at her in astonishment. Was this the little hippie of the morning? It didn't seem possible. The two girls studied each other frankly.

Marta laughed. "Clothes make a difference, don't they?

Sorry I had to throw you out of my room that way. Have you been able to make a reservation for the night somewhere?"

"I'll wait and see what Vance wants me to do."

"There's really no place for you here now, Page. I guess you didn't think of that when you persuaded me to come home." Marta settled herself in a chair before the empty grate. "How'd you happen to meet Vance?" she asked.

"His boss and my father were great friends. So we naturally met in San Francisco."

"Somehow," Marta said, "Vance never has struck me as the kind of man who would want a girl another man had discarded." She turned her head sharply. "Oh, I didn't hear you come in."

"So I gathered," Vance said evenly. "When did you get here?"

"This afternoon. I've been telling Page I'm sorry to kick her out of my room but, after all —"

"She can have mine," Vance said.

"I don't think she'd care to drive you out of your own house," Marta said. "She can go to a hotel."

"She'll stay here. And I'm staying here too. For the next few nights I'm going to sleep on this couch." Vance watched his young cousin, saw the color fade out of her face. "Just what do you think you are trying to do, Marta?"

"Nothing," she said sullenly. "I should think you'd be glad to have me back instead of being so mean."

The telephone rang and Vance answered it. The man at the other end of the wire talked for a long time. Vance looked across the room at Marta.

"So we've pinned down one thing at least," he said in a tone of satisfaction. "Jerome Brooks was the courier three months ago, and he went to Greece. But why did the fool let himself be involved . . . Yes, I know he needed money but, good lord, man, he wanted it to further his diplomatic career . . . Yes, I suppose they develop a sixth sense about the men who are for sale."

When he had set down the telephone he said to Marta, "Oh no. You aren't going to telephone. You aren't going to leave this house. We've got Brooks where we want him and you aren't going to warn him."

"What are you going to do to him?"

"At best, his hope of a career is dead. He'll be lucky if he can get out of the country, probably head back for Greece before we pick him up."

Marta crossed the room running, clawed at his sleeve. "You can't do that, Vance! You can't! I've got to see him. I've got to."

He shook his head. "Brooks won't want to see you again, Marta. You've served your purpose."

NINETEEN

"I DON'T like this any better than you do, Aunt Jane," Vance said, "but right now there is too much at stake. I think Marta came home — was sent home — to get Page out of the house, to make her — vulnerable. That's why I slept on the couch here last night."

"What have you done with Marta?"

"She is locked in her room," Vance said bluntly. He held out the key. "There are only two choices, Aunt Jane. Either you keep the key and see that Marta neither leaves the house nor telephones, or I'll have to send a security operative from Markham's to take over."

"Oh, no, that would be unbearable. I'll see that Marta stays here." Unexpectedly tears spilled down Mrs. Wentley's cheeks. "But when I do that I will have lost the last hope of winning back my daughter's love or her respect. She will never forgive me."

Vance covered her hand with his for a moment and then got up. "If you are sure you can manage without help, I'll be on my way. If anything comes up that you don't know how to deal with, call me at the office."

"I'll manage."

When Page's tray was brought up, Mrs. Wentley said, "Miss Wilburn is in Mr. Cooper's room until we can make other arrangements." But when Marta's arrived, she had it placed on a table, waited until Perkins had gone downstairs, and then unlocked the door to Marta's room and carried in the tray herself.

The girl lay smoldering. "I didn't think you would make me a prisoner."

"Only for a few days," her mother said. "Only —"

"If I want to get out you can't stop me."

"If you make the slightest effort to get out or get in touch with anyone Vance will have someone here to see that you remain in your own room."

"He has no right — you have no right —"

Mrs. Wentley put the tray across Marta's knees, went out and turned the key in the lock.

She was pacing up and down the sitting room when Page came out of Vance's room. "Vance made me lock Marta in," she said.

"You understand why, don't you, Aunt Jane? She must not be allowed to get in touch with Jerry. It won't be long now. Maybe the whole thing will end today."

"Long enough to destroy the last vestige of Marta's affection for me." Mrs. Wentley started nervously as the telephone rang.

"Mrs. Wentley, this is Beverly."

"Oh!" After a moment Mrs. Wentley managed to say steadily, "How are you, my dear?"

"I'm feeling so ashamed! I don't know what got into me. I was jealous, I guess. Anyhow, I'd like to make up for the horrible things I said if I can. Where has Page gone, do you know?"

"Gone? Why she is right here."

The girl at the other end of the wire caught her breath in surprise.

Mrs. Wentley put her hand over the telephone, shaped

the words, "Kate Willing," and held out the telephone.

"This is Page Wilburn, Miss Main."

"My dear, I haven't congratulated you properly on your engagement. And I do want to know you better."

Page's eyebrows arched in astonishment as she looked at Mrs. Wentley.

"And," the girl gushed on, "I'm so devoted to my god-mother, of course, that I feel we're all part of the same family. I'm wondering if you can lunch with me today, so that we can really begin to get acquainted."

Page hesitated, considering and discarding various alternatives. Then she said, "Of course. I'd be delighted."

"At one? At the Beekman? I'm afraid I'm not giving you much notice."

"I had no plans," Page told her and put down the telephone. When she had reported the conversation, Mrs. Wentley exclaimed, "No, you mustn't, Page. It may be some kind of trap."

"Perhaps, though I don't see what harm can come to me in the lobby or restaurant of a midtown hotel. Anyhow, I'm chaperoned, you know, by those two security agents, and this may be the only possible way in which we can find out what the girl is trying to accomplish. If she is after the pendant she can't have it. If it's anything else — well, it's better to know. She may give away her hand. But if I'm not back by — oh, half-past three, you'd better call Vance. He'll know what to do."

There was a touch of frost in the air, and Page was grateful for the warm black coat she had bought. As there was plenty of time she decided to walk to the hotel, so there would be no risk of her escorts' losing her by failing to get a taxi. She had told Vance the truth when she said she didn't feel brave. On the other hand, there was nothing to fear about this public lunch engagement and she was wildly curious. She walked swiftly, wondering why Marta had suddenly reversed her stand and come home, why Kate was pretending to be so friendly. On the whole she agreed with Vance that there was a determined effort to get her out of the Murray Hill house, away from her protectors.

Obviously Kate Willing had been surprised to find she was still there. It seemed likely that Marta's instructions had been to get rid of her at all costs. Again Page felt a thrill of anger when she remembered the clothes Marta had flung on the floor in Vance's room.

The girl who had called herself Beverly Main was waiting in the hotel lobby. She smiled at Page. "How lovely of you to come," she gushed. "I'm afraid we got off on the wrong foot. I was jealous of you, as I suppose you know, but now I do want us to be friends." She led the way to the restaurant.

"And how is dear Mrs. Wentley?" The sharp eyes studied Page carefully.

"Just fine," she assured her. "Something wonderful has happened. Her daughter Marta has come home."

"Oh? I didn't know she had a daughter."

"But you mentioned her the night Vance and I reached New York. Don't you remember?" Page was smiling, casual. "You said you had expected to have Marta's room."

"Oh, I — I suppose Vance must have spoken of her, but I'd forgotten. I've never seen the girl."

Page looked around idly, saw a waiter draw out a chair

at a nearby table for a girl who gave her a quick nod and a smile. It was nice to know that there was someone near at hand, someone looking out for her.

"I'm afraid," her hostess said unhappily, "you don't like me, and I do so want you to like me. Won't you call me Beverly?"

I wonder, Page thought in amusement, what would happen if I suggested calling her Kate?

"Do you see anything that looks good?" her hostess asked, and Page brought back her wayward thoughts and ordered lunch.

"I suppose," Kate said, "Mrs. Wentley told you those awful things I said about your jade pendant. But honestly it looked like the one that was advertised. I feel just terrible — practically accusing you — I see you aren't wearing it today."

"Not with this blue dress," Page said.

"Someday I would like to have a chance to study it. Not," Kate added hastily, "because I still have that crazy idea, but because it's so beautiful."

"Of course."

The soup had been served when a bellboy came in, saying in the monotonous chant of people calling names in hotels, "Miss Wilburn, please. Telephone call for Miss Wilburn."

That would be Vance wanting to be sure she was all right. Only Mrs. Wentley had known where she was going, and she must have called him at once. She murmured an excuse, heard a polite, "Oh, of course," and followed the boy out into the lobby.

Kate Willing finished her soup, dispatched her main course without waiting for her guest, refused dessert but sat in a leisurely way over coffee. Not, however, as though she were waiting for anyone. Then, humming lightly to herself, she went out, glanced around the empty lobby, smiled, and took the elevator to her room.

She turned the key in the lock, stepped inside, stopped short. "Who are you and what are you doing here?" she asked, her voice loud and frightened.

ii

In the lobby the bellboy, instead of indicating the whereabouts of the telephone, nodded toward the waiting man who came forward eagerly to take Page's arm.

"Jerry!"

He was white. His eyes were sunken. His voice shook. "Page, I had to see you."

"This is absurd. I've told you there was nothing left for us to say to each other. How did you know where I was? And why should you come to find me?"

"In the words of the old melodramas it's a matter of life and death," he said, and there was no mockery in his voice, only deadly seriousness.

"It's too late, Jerry," she told him. "Much too late. Nothing can be changed now. I suppose Marta got to a telephone, after all, to tell you I'd be here."

"Marta?" His eyes wavered. "I don't know what you are talking about."

"Or was it Kate Willing? I know about you and Marta and Kate."

"I might have known Marta couldn't keep her mouth shut. Look here, we can't talk in this place. Can't you give me ten minutes? I'll never ask anything of you again."

The outer door opened, letting a wave of chilly air into

the overheated lobby. Four men came in, a bellboy ran to collect luggage; there was a general bustle as the newcomers moved toward the desk.

Automatically stepping back out of their way Page saw the young man who appeared to have completed a telephone call. He looked from her to Jerry, gave her a faint nod, and turned away, moving unobtrusively toward the door. Evidently he intended to follow them.

"All right," Page agreed. "I suppose your friend Kate will know I'm not coming back to finish lunch."

The doorman hailed the taxi which had just unloaded the four men and Jerry helped her in. She turned in the seat to see the unobtrusive young man get into the next taxi in line, so she failed to hear the address which Jerry gave in a low voice.

Then he turned the full effect of his charming smile on Page.

"My lovely darling," he said softly.

Because of the noise of traffic he had to raise his voice and repeat so that his words were almost shouted, which spoiled their effect. Bumper-to-bumper traffic moved in a blare of horns, throbbing of motors. The wail of an ambulance siren forced traffic to pull to the side. Then it surged on again.

"You can't really understand, can you, Jerry, that it just doesn't work any more. You never loved me. You've never loved anyone but yourself. So let's not waste time pretending. You don't want me. What do you want?"

"You just can't forgive me." He still could not believe that his charm would not work.

"No, I can't forgive you, but it's not because of what you did to me. That doesn't even matter any more. In fact, when

I think I might have married you instead of Vance I can't be grateful enough for my escape."

"What has he got that's so wonderful?"

"Qualities you wouldn't understand: loyalty, honor, simple human kindness."

The taxi had stopped before a rather shabby four-story apartment building that had seen better days and that looked ill at ease among its more prosperous neighbors. Somewhat to Page's surprise Jerry, after helping her out of the cab, indicated the area steps.

"I've got a little place in the basement," he said. "Cheaper down there." He sounded rather bitter.

As she preceded him down the stairs she glanced back automatically. There was no sign of the cab with her escort. Somewhere in traffic he had lost her. Page stopped short, but Jerry had her arm, swept her inside the basement, unlocked a door. When she was inside he locked it again, put the key in his pocket, and stood looking at her, his eyes very bright.

"I'm sorry," he said, "for all this melodrama, but you'll have to give it to me, you know."

"Give you what?" she asked, knowing quite well what his answer would be.

"That jade figurine."

"I don't have it."

"Oh, yes, you do. It isn't in the house on Murray Hill. Where is it? Under your dress?"

She put out a hand to hold him off. "No, I'm not wearing it, Jerry."

"I've got to have it."

She shook her head.

"I tell you —" He caught her arm, drew her toward him.

She made no attempt to resist. The deep blue eyes met his sadly. "I don't have it, Jerry."

Something in her tone, in her expression, made him step back. His hand dropped to his side.

"And even if I had," she went on, "it wouldn't do you any good. The microfilm has been found and turned over to the security branch at Markham's."

Something in Jerry's good-looking face seemed to collapse. He leaned against the door, no longer as though he were guarding it but as though his knees had folded and he could not hold himself upright without support.

"How," she cried, "could you have involved yourself in a thing like this? You had a dazzling career ahead of you. You've thrown away everything. For what?"

"I had to have the money to get ahead," he said almost angrily. "I had to have it. And your father had lost everything. And — when the subject came up —"

"When it was suggested that you become a traitor to your country," Page said hotly.

Dark color stained his face, ebbed again. "It wasn't like that. I was just asked to make a trip to Greece, to take an unusual cigarette case with a built-in lighter to a guy over there. It was all so easy. I was to show the case, a man was to say, 'Miracle the way they make these things, isn't it?' I'd get ten thousand dollars."

"And you didn't care about what might be hidden in the cigarette case?"

"What's the use of talking about it?" He was sullen. "You wouldn't understand. I am ambitious to get ahead. I suppose they recognized that."

Page laughed. "Come out of your dream world, Jerry. Last night when Vance learned about your acting as courier he said, 'I suppose they have a sixth sense about the men who are for sale.' " Even as she said it she knew she had made a mistake. Jerry could live only with his ideal picture of himself. He would never accept or forgive the truth.

"You've been in my way all the time, haven't you, Page? You've been the stumbling block. First you ran out of money. Then you blundered onto the password and got the pendant. Then you kept Kate out of the Murray Hill house. Always in the way."

Something different was happening to his face now. Something ugly was stirring behind his eyes. And Page was afraid, more afraid than she had ever been in her life. It's Jerry, she told herself, only Jerry. He — couldn't hurt me. He — wouldn't hurt me. But she wished the operative had not lost her taxi. She wished the woman in the restaurant had followed her. She wished Vance knew where she was.

"What got you into this?" she asked. "Oh, Jerry, how could you?"

He started to speak. Stopped abruptly. He pulled away from the door and he was walking slowly toward her.

Insensibly Page was moving back, step by step, as he advanced.

"Always in the way," he said again. "And they don't excuse failure. They say — the word has gone out —"

"You wouldn't hurt me," she whispered.

He avoided her eyes.

"Jerry, come one step closer and I'll scream."

"Go ahead. There's no one on the first two floors all day long. The superintendent lives two buildings away. And what with traffic — go ahead —"

"Why?" She had stepped back again. "Why?"

"Because these people play for keeps. They don't forget blunders. They can't afford to forget blunders."

"You've blundered?"

"That woman in the brown coat — the one who heard you use the password and put the pendant in a box for you — she tried to get it back when she found it should have gone to Kate, but it was too late. Yesterday," Jerry's tongue touched dry lips, "she was run over in San Francisco. That's what happens when you make mistakes. And then you messed things up for me. Kept Kate out of the Wentley house. It's too late to get the pendant now but —"

"But why do they want me to die?" Page demanded, and then answered her own question. "Oh! Of course. Because he would have known where it was. He was following me. And then — he went ahead and waited . . . Jerry! Before you do something you can't — change, something that will spoil the rest of your life — give it up. Cut your losses. Tell the truth and take your medicine. That will be better than what will happen to you otherwise. Anything will be better."

"It's you or me now," Jerry said steadily. "That's all the choice there is."

"But they know," Page told him. "Vance knows. The Markham people know. About you. It's too late, Jerry."

"I can still get out," he said. "They'll manage to send me to Greece. From there on, I'll be taken care of."

"Would you really trust him that far?"

"Trust whom?" Jerry asked.

"The man who bought you, the man who is trying to sell out his country, his company, the employees who trust him? The man who ordered you to kill me. The man who tried to kill me himself. Miles Forrest."

As Jerry lunged toward her she screamed. Then he jerked around as a key grated in the lock and the door swung open. Facing them, a revolver in his hand, was the ferret-faced man.

TWENTY

"SHE asked me to wait until half-past three and if she hadn't come by then to get in touch with you," Mrs. Wentley said, "but I'm afraid to take the chance. I thought I had better call you at once."

"She should never have gone," Vance told her. "You shouldn't have let her go."

"How could I stop her? And she felt safe because of her two chaperons, as she calls them. Anyhow, she thought there might be a chance of learning something about Bev — Kate Willing."

"Is Marta still in her room?"

"Yes."

"Has she been able to get at the telephone?"

"No. Marta has nothing to do with this, Vance. Oh, there's one thing. When this girl — when Kate telephoned, she was obviously surprised to find that Page was still here. I think," Mrs. Wentley tried to speak steadily, "it must have been Marta's job to see that Page was driven out."

"Try not to worry, Aunt Jane," Vance said and put down the telephone.

Try not to worry. Page had walked into the lion's den. My crazy darling, he thought, why didn't I lock you up too? I thought you had too much sense to take chances. Then, remembering her steady eyes, he knew that when she had taken the risk she had been aware of what she was doing.

He pulled the telephone toward him, called the security head, talked fast.

The poor devil, the security man thought in compassion, he's taking this hard.

"It's all right, Mr. Cooper," he said, "we have two operatives right with Miss Wilburn all the time. They won't risk losing sight of her for a single minute. We'll get word to the operative who is shadowing Kate Willing to be on the alert, though I can't see what could possibly happen to the girl in the lobby or restaurant of a midtown hotel."

Vance tried to work, found he could concentrate on nothing. The telephone rang. It was the head of security.

"Jane, the operative we had at the Forrest apartment followed Miss Wilburn to the Beekman. She will get a table as near hers as possible. Everything is under control. Our other operative is out in the lobby. He just called in."

Try not to worry. The words were bitter on Vance's lips and he tried to reason with himself. Two people were watching Page, one of them probably within a few feet of her. Nonetheless he felt in his bones that somewhere they had slipped up.

The telephone rang again. The security man was grim. "Bad news," he said succinctly. "Miss Wilburn was paged in the restaurant. Jerome Brooks was waiting for her in the lobby. Joe Lamb, our operative, took the next taxi, but he got held up in traffic. He —"

"He's lost her," Vance said bleakly.

"He — well, yes."

"There's something else, isn't there?"

"Well," and this time the security man sounded defeated, "no point in beating around the bush. Joe saw that ferret-faced man. He was in a private car that had been waiting. He was right behind the taxi with the Wilburn girl and Brooks. That's the way the breaks go at times."

"You don't know where Brooks lives?"

"No." He added defensively, "We just don't have that many men. It would take an army to cover everyone."

Vance set down the telephone. Then he pushed back his chair, flung open the door, ran down the corridor, shouting as an elevator door was closing, crowded in.

On the street he hailed a cab and gave the Murray Hill address. "And hurry," he said. "For God's sake, hurry. I'll pay the fine, if necessary."

He thrust a ten-dollar bill into the driver's hand and opened the door before the latter could turn around. He had his key in the lock, was racing up the circular staircase.

Mrs. Wentley had risen to her feet, she was staring at him. "Vance! What is wrong?"

"Give me the key to Marta's room."

She handed it to him without a word; he unlocked the door and flung it open. Marta was sitting at the window, wearing rose silk pajamas and a matching robe. She turned sullenly to glare at Vance.

He crossed the room, seized her by the shoulders, drew her to her feet.

"Where does Jerome Brooks live?" he asked.

"I don't know."

"You're lying!" He shook her. "Marta! Where! I've got to know at once. At once, you understand?"

"You wouldn't let me talk to him. Why should I let you do it?"

"I'll tell you why. He has kidnaped Page Wilburn. That's

why he sent you here, isn't it, to drive her out of this house, to make it easier for them to get hold of her."

Mrs. Wentley gave a little gasp of pain and stood, eyes closed, swaying.

"Marta!" Vance's hands tightened on her thin shoulders.

"You are hurting me," she said petulantly.

"What do you think they are doing to Page? They won't let her go. They don't dare let her go. There has already been one attempt to kill her. Marta, unless you speak now, you'll be guilty of Page's death. Do you understand?"

And Mrs. Wentley spoke then. "Page told me," she said, her voice cracked, like that of a very old woman, "that, in the long run, she was sure you could never do anything really bad."

Vance held his breath. And then Marta said, "Jerry has a basement apartment on East Fifty-fourth Street. I — oh, hurry, Vance! Hurry!"

He was already at the telephone in the sitting room, and then his feet hammered down the stairs.

"Oh, Mother," Marta said. "Oh, Mother!" This time it was she who held out her arms. At last Marta had come home.

ii

There was no movement at all in the basement apartment. All three seemed to be fixed in their positions like figures in a frieze.

Then the man with the gun said, "All right, Brooks."

Page's heart hammered, then it beat slowly and sluggishly, then it hammered. For days and days this man had followed her like a buzzard following a man lost on the desert. And now at last he had reached his objective. But the man did not even look at her. He was watching Jerry.

"All right," he said again. There was a metallic click and then there were handcuffs on Jerry's wrists. And now the man turned to Page. He was smiling. "All right, Miss Wilburn." All right seemed to be his favorite words. "Everything is fine now. You can go home. Sorry you were let in for this. I got held up by that ambulance, and if I hadn't guessed where Brooks would bring you —" He shook his head. "I hate to think of what Mr. Markham would have done to me."

"Mr. Markham!" Page's eyes widened. "Why you must be his star agent."

In her relief she sank onto a chair. She tried not to see Jerry's face, wearing an oddly shriveled look as though the life had drained out of it, tried not to see Jerry's hands held awkwardly in front of him.

"Come along." There was no kindness in the agent's voice now. Only contempt.

"Who are you and where are you taking me?" Jerry's bluster wasn't convincing.

"We'll have a nice little chat with the District Attorney," the agent said. "And you ought to thank heaven for that, Brooks. Your own crowd wouldn't let you get out of this room alive and you know it."

"I don't know what you are talking about."

The agent laughed. "Well, now, I hate to see a young man kept in the dark that way. You forced Miss Wilburn to come here —"

"Miss Wilburn and I are engaged," Jerry said, and gave her an imploring look. She wouldn't fail him now. She couldn't. No woman could resist his charm.

"Look here, Brooks," the agent said, "you don't even know the score. We've got that microfilm safe. We've got Kate Willing; at least, if she hasn't already been arrested she will be as soon as she goes back to her room. We know you were the first courier. We know she was to be the second. We've got her passport for Portugal. We know who hired you both. I must say she's a better bargainer than you are, must have made a lot more out of trying to sell her country down the river. What was your take? Couldn't have been much more than ten thousand. She got that much in cash, a mink jacket, and an expensive apartment for three months. A very good bargain indeed."

The agent watched Jerry with detachment but without sympathy. "Kate will talk, you know. The ship is going down and you know how rats are. They desert. She'll talk, no doubt of that. Though we don't need much more information than we have. We don't need a pointing finger because we've found our key man. Miles Forrest. Actually I've been on to him from the time in San Francisco when he tried to snatch that jade pendant from Miss Wilburn. Matter of fact, I saw him do it. But we needed a lot more evidence before we could move. You guessed, didn't you, Miss Wilburn?"

"Not then. But that night at his party, when he tried to throw me over the parapet," her eyes closed, she shook her head as though trying to drive away a nightmare, "and his ring cut my mouth in the same way, I began to wonder. There were little things. He kept saying we had met in Chinatown and actually he had asked me how to get there. When I realized he knew San Francisco well I knew he hadn't needed to ask. I thought then he had been following me to make sure I was wearing the pendant, then went ahead and waited for a chance to grab it. He knew that, sooner or later, I'd let slip how we had really met. So I was a danger to him. And Mrs. Forrest knew something was wrong. She — that night I think she was frightened. She suspected something when the lights went out. She knew something had happened. Anyhow, Mr. Forrest was overdoing that business of protecting Norman Graham."

"He'd have set Graham up as the villain of the piece if it hadn't been for your faith in him. I failed you there, Miss Wilburn. I was on the roof of the penthouse at the time the lights went out but I — Forrest moved so fast that if his wife hadn't called when she did, I couldn't have saved you. Nothing could have saved you."

"How much does she know?"

They were speaking as though Jerry were not there.

"She suspects. They have really been deeply in love for the eight years of their marriage, so far as anyone can find out. She'd be aware when something went wrong. Forrest had too much money: that penthouse, his general style of living. And, of course, he was paying out money to scum like Kate Willing and our friend Brooks here. We know Mrs. Forrest went to see her husband's broker to ask about their finances and found out he had carefully put everything in her name. Yes, I think the poor woman knows something is terribly wrong, and it's not difficult to tie up the trouble with Operation Homebase."

The agent took Jerry's arm. "Come on. We're going places."

Jerry, with his invincible faith in his charm, cried imploringly, "Page!"

She shook her head. "No, Jerry."

There was a rush of feet and the door was flung open. Vance came hurtling into the room followed by two men. He hurled himself at the agent.

"Vance," Page cried, "it's all right. This is Mr. Markham's crack agent."

The agent was showing his credentials to the others and apparently there was a good deal of mirth.

"But why didn't you tell us?" one of them demanded.

"Mr. Markham had reached the point where he wasn't taking chances on anyone."

Vance had reached Page, had pulled her into his arms. They tightened around her. His cheek pressed against the soft honey-colored hair, against a warm cheek, and then he found her lips.

"Have you been hurt?" he asked at length when he had lifted his mouth reluctantly from hers.

"Just scared. I told you I'm not heroine stuff."

"Do you need her here?" Vance asked.

The agent shook his head. "Take her away. It's all over." His face shadowed. "Except picking up the pieces."

He jerked at Jerry's arm and Jerry stumbled forward. For a moment he and Vance met each other's eyes and Jerry's fell. Then Vance, holding Page with an arm around her shoulders, took her out of the basement and up into the street.

By mutual consent they began to walk slowly west, jostled by crowds of people whom they did not notice, ignoring stop-and-go signs at street corners and unaware of their danger, walking in a no-man's-land inhabited by no one but themselves.

"I love you," Vance was saying. "I thought — for

twenty whole minutes I thought I had lost you. The worst twenty minutes of my life. Page, I can't ever lose you again. When will you marry me?"

"The very day Operation Homebase is completed."

"But that may mean waiting two or three weeks!" he protested.

She laughed. "When we get married I want your undivided attention." Looking into his eyes, she bumped into a mailbox, apologized politely to it, and went on.

Being a man he had to have it in words. "You've never said it," he insisted.

"I love you, Vance. I love you. Ouch!" as he steered her into the side of a parked car.

He caught her hand, laughing. "We'd better get home while we are all in one piece," he declared.

iii

"Miss Willing?" the man said politely.

Kate backed toward the door, groped for the knob.

"You are under arrest."

"You have made a mistake. My name is Main. Beverly Main."

He shook his head. "The mistake is yours, lady. Let's go downtown and have a nice long talk about your plans. They don't include a trip to Portugal, lady. Where you are going you won't need a passport."

She looked from one bland face to the other. "What kind of people are you? Breaking into a girl's room? When the management learns of this —"

"You want to see our credentials, lady?" One of the men flipped open his wallet, held it out. "You want to get your coat? Pack a bag maybe?"

"I'm not going anywhere," Kate said. "If you take me out of this room you'll never find out —"

"What happened to Miss Wilburn?" one of them said smoothly. "You'd better be sure that nothing happens to her, lady."

"At least I have the right to make a telephone call."

"To Miles Forrest?"

Kate stared at him and the color drained out of her face.

"Mr. Forrest will have other things on his mind right now than looking after your interests, lady."

"And stop calling me lady."

"I know," the man said sympathetically. "It sounds kind of funny to me, too."

iv

Ruth Forrest, her footsteps muffled by the deep pile of the carpet, walked down the hall and opened the door of her husband's bedroom. There was a suitcase on his bed into which he was folding a suit. A briefcase was propped on a chair, with an overcoat and a hat.

She stood watching him, a pretty dark-haired woman in a smart black dress, a diamond clip at the shoulder. There was love and grief and shame in her face as she watched the big bronzed man with his look of the out-of-doors, the man who had such promise, the college football hero, the brilliant engineer, the lover and husband and companion of eight happy years.

He had turned to open a drawer, to take out shirts. Still without moving she said quietly, "Where is it to be this time, Miles?"

He started, turned around to stare at her. "Ruth! I didn't

hear you. Sorry to have to dash off without warning. I've had a rush call from Markham in San Francisco."

"Have you, Miles?"

They were watching each other now.

He made a slight gesture, opened the closet, took down a tie rack.

"How long do you think it will be this time?" she asked.

"I can't tell." He was bending over the suitcase, his voice somewhat muffled. "Just a few days, I hope. Maybe longer."

"Maybe after Thanksgiving?"

"Well — if it should be that long I'll arrange to have you join me."

"You'll need me, won't you?"

He straightened at that, turned to gather her to him. "I always need you, Ruth."

For a moment she clung to him, and then she pushed him away. "But you need more than that, don't you, Miles? The money that is invested in my name."

His face had hardened.

"I wanted to know how we managed to spend so much money, so much more than your salary. I went to see your broker. He has invested an enormous amount for you, hasn't he, Miles?"

"I've done well," he admitted.

"Have you?"

"Very well." He managed a hearty tone. "They say you can't beat Wall Street, but I've really made a killing. The reason I've put the stuff, so much of it, in your name, is on account of taxes, of course."

"Is it, Miles?"

"Well, after all, people do it all the time."

"And you want me to bring it to you? Egypt, isn't it? I found your passport yesterday."

And now husband and wife faced each other.

"What on earth," he began, trying to bluff, trying to laugh.

"The information that leaked out to the enemy about Operation Homebase — you're responsible, aren't you, Miles? I think, in a way, I've known all along. You can't love a person with all your heart for eight years and not come to know what he is like. I knew something was wrong, just as I've known we were spending too much money. I didn't want all this —" She made a gesture. "The penthouse, the jewelry, the clothes by Dior. All I wanted was you."

"But I wanted you to have them," he said.

She shook her head. "No, you wanted them for yourself. Blatant, obvious signs of—" her voice broke, "I suppose you'd call it success."

Miles looked out of the window at the gleaming towers of the city. "Anyone would call it success. What are you worrying about, Sweetheart?"

"About the things that have gone wrong."

"Nothing has gone wrong."

"I knew something was wrong about the Wilburn girl and young Graham. I knew you weren't acting like yourself. You aren't normally that way; you don't usually point out to everyone what a loyal fellow you are. So I — wondered why it should be necessary now."

"Look here, Ruth —" He caught sight of the clock on the desk and reached hastily for handkerchiefs, shorts, stuffed them into the suitcase. "There's no time to explain now. I'll write you about the whole thing. I'll tell you where to meet me and how to arrange things."

"Miles, you must listen to me. I won't meet you anywhere out of this country. If you go away — escape —
defect to the enemy — you must do it alone. I have loved
you as much as it is possible for a woman to love. I still do.
But there could be no trust between us ever again. No confidence. No respect."

"Ruth!"

She shook her head.

"You'll change your mind." He was confident about
that. "I'll write and explain the whole thing. Tell you what
to do about the money. Where to join me." He locked the
suitcase, pulled on his overcoat, picked up the briefcase. "I
know this is a shock, Sweetheart, but you are too sensible,
we mean too much to each other —" The clock chimed and
he hurried out.

His wife dropped onto a chair. "Good-bye, Miles," she
whispered. "Good-bye, my darling. God help you!"

She did not cry. Her grief was too deep for the relief of
tears. She was still sitting there, numbed with pain, when
Miles Forrest's taxi drew up at the airport. Picking up
suitcase and briefcase he started toward the big building.
Two men closed in, one on either side.

"Going somewhere, Mr. Forrest?" one of them asked
politely.

TWENTY-ONE

THE KITCHEN of the house on Murray Hill was filled with the appetizing smell of roasting turkey as Mrs. Perkins opened the oven. She nodded. "You can take it out now."

Perkins lifted the huge bird onto a platter while his wife watched breathless for fear of catastrophe. Then she expelled a long sigh of relief.

"It must be five years," Perkins said, "since Mrs. Wentley has had an old-fashioned Thanksgiving like this, with the turkey carved at the table and all."

"This year," his wife said, "there's more to be thankful for than ever before. There's more happiness in this house than I can remember." She tasted the oyster stuffing. "Just perfect," she said in satisfaction and then filled a gravy boat, slid cranberry jelly into glass bowls, and mashed the potatoes and turnips until they were fluffy.

Perkins took butterballs off the ice and removed long dishes of celery and olives from the refrigerator. "Are the creamed onions ready?"

"Everything is ready. But don't announce dinner until after the President's speech. They'll all be listening and it's just time now."

In the small sitting room behind the kitchen, Perkins switched on their television set. "The following interview was recorded yesterday," the announcer said. "Ladies and gentlemen, the President of the United States."

Beside the President stood Horace Markham. The President spoke briefly but warmly, extending his personal congratulations and expressing the gratitude of the American people for the brilliant achievement of the Markham Electronics Company and its contribution to the space race.

"This year, Mr. Markham," he concluded, "you have given us all something for which to be deeply thankful."

"Mr. President," Markham said, "my part in the success of Operation Homebase has been a minor one. That success is the result of the loyal teamwork of the whole organization. For months the people at Markham's have devoted all their time and energy to a single goal. They have sacrificed their leisure. In some cases," and he smiled faintly, "they have nearly shipwrecked their private lives. In a few cases," and he did not smile at all, "they have risked their lives for the welfare of us all. While there are such people, Mr. President, we can indeed be grateful and thankful."

Perkins shut off the set. "It's the first time," he told his wife, "that I've really understood about Thanksgiving's being a symbol of the triumph of human courage over obstacles." He went out to the drawing room, caught Mrs. Wentley's eye. "Dinner is served."

She smiled and laid her hand on the arm of the man with the leonine head. "We feel very proud at having you with us, Mr. Markham."

It was a small party but a gay one. Vance and Page, who was starry-eyed with happiness; Norman Graham and his fiancée, Helen, who had flown east from San Francisco to

renew their engagement and celebrate Thanksgiving; Marta
and the gay young engineer whom Page had found such
fun at the Forrest dinner party.

Mrs. Wentley looked happily from face to face, but the
one on which her eyes lingered longest was that of her
daughter Marta, a gentler Marta, a Marta without de-
fiance, a Marta who was responding rather shyly to the
jokes of the young engineer. He was far from being the
professional charmer Jerry Brooks had been, but he was
without pretensions, and it was clear that he found Marta
attractive. She was vivid now that she was happy. She listened to something the young engineer was saying, her face
alight with laughter.

If he should want to marry her, Mrs. Wentley thought,
he'll probably hesitate because of the money. How can I —
can we — her eyes rested on Page. Page will know what to
do, what to say, she thought, and again her heart swelled
with the spirit of thanksgiving.

She remembered when Vance had brought Page home
two weeks ago. For over an hour she and Marta had waited
in tense silence and anguish after Vance's frantic rush down
the stairs. Then at last he had returned, bringing Page safe
and sound.

Marta had stood at the top of the staircase, her eyes
enormous in her white face. "Oh, thank God," she had
whispered. "Page, can you forgive me?"

"It's all over now," Page had told her. "It's the past.
Let's forget it and start over. Shall we?"

Helen's voice rang out over the dinner table. "What on
earth are you people going to do with yourselves now you've
completed Operation Homebase?"

"You and I," Norman said, "are going apartment hunting."

"In that Cadillac or in a Volkswagen?"

"From now on, my girl," he assured her darkly, "you'll be riding subways."

This book has been read
by:-

Barbara Zahn --- January 1970
Mary Dietmear ---- Summer 1971
Barbara Zahn ----- January 1973